Delicate

Also by Steph Campbell

GROUNDING QUINN

Delicate

Steph Campbell

SIMON AND SCHUSTER

First published in Great Britain in 2012 as eBook original
by Simon and Schuster UK Ltd
This paperback edition published in 2013 by Simon and Schuster UK Ltd
A CBS COMPANY

1 3 5 7 9 10 8 6 4 2

Simon & Schuster UK Ltd
1st Floor
222 Gray's Inn Road
London WC1X 8HB

Simon & Schuster Australia, Sydney
Simon & Schuster India, New Delhi

A CIP catalogue record for this book is available
from the British Library.

eBook ISBN: 978-1-47111-758-9
PB ISBN: 978-1-47111-759-6

Printed and bound by CPI Group (UK) Ltd, Croydon, CR0 4YY

www.simonandschuster.co.uk
www.simonandschuster.com.au

For Monica.
For forcing me to read 'that book' all those years ago.
It got me not only reading again – it got me writing.
(And for introducing me to Damien).
I love you like family. Always.

One

"Where should I look?" I ask.

Jeff, the tech who has been setting filming equipment up in my house all day, looks at me with exasperated eyes.

"Sorry, I've just never done anything like this before," I say.

He lets out a long sigh, signalling that he likely thinks I'm the stupidest person alive. "The camera is here," he says, pointing to the small camera mounted to the wall of the makeshift "confessional booth", which is actually just our porch. The walls have been filled in, and the porch swings replaced with a large, comfortable chair that has my trophies and medals arranged behind it. Gold ones up front, of course.

"So, looking *there* would probably be a good idea," he finishes.

"Right," I nod. I'm trying to be polite, but Jeff here is making it awfully difficult.

"So, here's what we're going to need from you," he continues. "At least once a day, you're going to have to set aside some time to come in here and talk for about thirty minutes. Just sit down and press this button." He points to a small black remote. "Tell us what you did at gym, tell us about school. If you took a test, we want to know. If you got asked out on a date, we want to know."

"I have a boyfriend already," I interrupt. "I mean, I won't be going out on a lot of dates."

1

"Boyfriend?" He flips through the small stack of pages on his clipboard. "That's not listed anywhere in your notes."

For a reason, Sydney. *Crap*.

"He's really private," I say.

"I see. Well, Ms Pierce, you signed away your right to privacy when you signed your contract. *You're* the one that applied to be a part of this documentary. Anything that we film is ours to use."

It's my turn to sigh. I'm the last person cut out for something like this. But when my best friend, Quinn, showed me the flyer for an upcoming documentary on young Olympic hopefuls, it was too good an opportunity to pass up. Elite gymnastics is pricey, and though my dad makes decent money, I just don't think that every cent he earns needs to go to on my coaching and travelling. Sure, I could take the prize money I win at competitions, but doing that would make me ineligible to compete in college, which is important if I want to get a scholarship. Plus who knows how long I'll be able to compete for – everyone knows this elite-level career has an expiration date. So, signing away my life for a couple of months sucks, but I know it will take some stress away from my dad, and after the last couple of years we've had, I'm willing to sacrifice a little privacy for him.

"The boyfriend is fair game. We want to hear everything, this romance stuff sells."

I nod, but I know that there's no way Trevor will go for being a part of this. He'd blown up at me when I told him I applied in the first place and it was only because my odds of being picked were so slim that things settled down. But now there are cameramen in my house doing test shots. They'll be showing up at school. They'll be at the gym with me this week. Yeah, now it's looking more real. *Ugh*. I wonder if it's too late to back out!

"Your school has only granted permission for us to film there two hours a week, so we're really limited on that stuff." Jeff says, interrupting my thoughts. "You'll definitely have to fill in some blanks. We all know that gymnastics takes up the majority of your time – but it's not everything. Just think of this like writing in your diary."

"I don't keep I diary," I say.

He rolls his eyes and wipes the sweat from his brow with the back of his hand.

"Look, kid, pretend. Give us something good. Keep people watching."

There isn't a more boring person alive. Quinn would have been perfect for this. She's witty. Sarcastic. *Fun*. That would be entertainment. But I don't exactly lead a normal teenage life. There aren't any parties, or wild nights out with friends. I go to gym twice a day – at five in the morning before school and then straight after school until six or seven in the evening. Then I come home, do my homework and crash out.

"So, let's give it a shot." Jeff says, "When you come in, just press this button, have a seat and talk about whatever comes to mind. Fake it, I don't care. Make it good, though."

Fake it.

Like when some stranger wants to talk about how Mom died and asks if it bothers me.

Fake it.

Like when I'm standing in the bronze medal place and a reporter asks how I feel about the gold medal winner.

Fake it.

Like when Dad asks if he's doing a good job on his own. If he's keeping things running like when Mom was here.

Fake it.

Like when Trevor holds my hand a little too hard when other

3

guys are around and I don't say anything, because that'd be admitting that I felt like something was wrong.

Fake it.

That's something I do know how to do.

Two

I readjust my hands on the uneven bar, gripping it tighter under my chalk-covered palms, knowing that I only have letting go left in the routine.

"Hurry up, Sydney," my coach, Sam, booms from below.

I swing my body up over the high bar, completing another full Giant Swing.

"Sydney, one more Giant and I will pull you down from the bar myself. Dis. Mount." Sam clips his last word and I know that he means business.

I know everyone has their hang-ups. Mine just happens to be more of a nemesis. It's called an Arabian Double Front – it's a half-twist into not one – but two front somersaults in the air, then landing without being able to spot the ground first., Lucky me, it's the skill that we're working on in this morning's session. I hate it – not in the way that I hate soggy french fries, humidity or the way I look in green – I mean, I *really* despise it. It's not that it's the most difficult gym skill by any means, but that doesn't stop me from nearly hyperventilating every time I do it. It's not a fear of heights, or the flipping multiple times, or even being afraid of getting hurt – I'm an elite gymnast, I've been training for years, I'm used to those things. No, for me, it's deeper than that. It's the anxiety that comes with letting go of the bar and landing blindly. It's the crippling feeling I have when I think about purposely giving up control, and not being able to see where I'm going to land when it's all over.

I hold my breath and fling my body away from the bar, tucking my legs as I flip. I spot the ground and lock my eyes on the blue mat, waiting for my feet to meet it.

They don't.

Instead, my heels slip as they slam into the mat and I lose my footing. I stumble backwards. One step, two, until I fall flat on to my back.

"That's gonna leave a bruise," Sam says, shaking his head as he walks away from me.

I pull the grips off of my hands and shove them into my duffel bag, knowing that Sam is exactly right, I knew before I even hit the ground that the fall is going to leave a nasty mark.

"Won't be the first, or the last," I mumble to no one.

Oh yeah, except the camera guy in my face.

"That was perfect," he says with a giddy smile.

It isn't even eight o'clock in the morning, and already the Georgia heat and humidity have plastered my hair to my face in frizzy waves. *Perfect.*

I pull my backpack off and rummage through the loose pencils, hoping for a hairband to pull my hair back into a ponytail with. No such luck.

Then Trevor, my boyfriend of just over a year, walks up behind me. I don't need to turn around to know it's him, I always smell his heavy cologne before I even see him.

"Morning, beautiful," he says.

I turn around and stand on my tip-toes to give him a quick kiss.

"How was gym?" he asks.

"It was good. I got a lot done," I lie. I can't tell him the truth. That that stupid skill paralyzes me every time.

It's not that Trevor doesn't get sports. He's really athletic too. But he's also fearless. Unlike me. I question everything. I'm always a little uncertain. Insecure. He wouldn't understand me letting one move get to me so much.

"Good," he says. "Next question. Did you talk to him yet?"

"Talk to who?" I ask.

Trevor runs his hand through his thick blond hair and lets out an annoyed sigh.

"Your dad, Sydney. Have you talked to your dad about the lake house?"

I try not to visibly wince. I was really hoping he wouldn't ask me about that again this week. I know I'd told him that I was ready to spend the night with him, but every time Trevor brings it up I have to remind myself *why* I said that. Am I *really* ready? Trevor's a senior, a year older than me, and his parents are letting him and some friends stay out at their lake house after prom this year. It seemed like the perfect idea when he first mentioned I should stay over. I *do* want to be with him, and really I don't know why I've put it off this long. Plus I've heard the comments when Trevor and I are together.

"Why is he even with her?"

"She doesn't even know what to do with a guy like him."

"I bet he's cheating on her."

I want to be closer to Trevor. *Closest.* To have something with him that will make me more secure in our relationship. To silence those whispers. But, God, I'm so nervous. Especially when it comes to having to lie to my dad.

"I'll talk to him tonight. I promise," I say.

"That's my girl," Trevor says. He picks up my hand and kisses each of my knuckles.

7

I met Trevor two years ago. I was dealing with the loss of my mom and shutting everyone I knew out. It was easier to do that than to have to try and constantly convince everyone that you were okay ... *really*. With everything going on at home, I hadn't turned in my schedule request on time at school, so I was stuck with Theatre Arts as an elective. Trevor and I were partnered up, and at first I could barely breathe around him, because he was just this hot, older guy. But even though he made me really nervous, he also made me laugh for the first time in months. For the longest time, I was scared to let him in in case he saw how totally broken I was and ran a mile. But that term, our relationship changed from a lighthearted friendship, to something more. I felt safe. And happy.

And *that* is why I agreed to the lake house.

"What are you thinking about?" Trevor asks.

"You. And how we're both going to be late," I say. I motion to the door of my Oceanography class.

Trevor lets out a smooth, sexy laugh that makes me smile.

"Fine, have it your way," he says, kissing my forehead before he turns away, waving casually over his shoulder.

I dive into the classroom and slide into my seat just as the bell rings. I like to be prepared, so getting to class at the last second makes me anxious. I quickly unpack my heavy textbook and ring binder and organise them neatly on the table. I don't know anyone in my first period class. In fact, I'm pretty certain no one in here even knows my first name. Mostly people just know me as Trevor's girlfriend. At the beginning of the year, a girl had been in the seat next to me, but she moved a couple of weeks in, leaving me alone on my own little island. But I don't mind.

I tap my pencil on the top of my binder, waiting for the lecture to begin. I really need an A in this class. If I can manage straight As again this term, Dad said he'll consider letting me home school so that I can go to the gym more often. I already go twice a day, but still, it can't hurt. Plus, I miss a ton of school as it is with competitions. Out of the corner of my eye, I see someone enter the room. He walks to the front of the room and hands something to our teacher Mrs Drez.

"All right, listen up," she says. Her raspy voice permanently sounds like she's in serious need of a Ricola. "This is Grant, obviously he's new. It'd be nice if you guys could do something for someone else for a change and show him around a bit. You know, help him out if needed."

A chorus of groans echoes through the room. Mrs Drez motions to the empty spot at my table, naturally, as it's the only free seat in the class.

Grant glances at me as he flops his book bag down on to the table. I smile politely, while squealing internally. Good lord, he's gorgeous! Not conventionally handsome like Trevor. But there is something about him. The curious way his hair goes every which way, and I can't tell if he woke up like that, or he spent hours perfecting it. Based on his v-neck t-shirt, jeans and Chucks, I'd go with the former. It isn't normal for me to even notice any other guy but Trevor. But as Grant slides into his chair, he bumps my arm lightly with his and immediately, heat rushes through me. I lock my eyes on Mrs Drez, and bite my lip to stop myself saying or doing anything stupid.

Somehow, I manage to make it through the hour with my dignity intact. As soon as I hear the bell ring, I rush out of the room. I've just crossed the doorway and into the safe zone of the corridor, and am about to head down the stairs to my next class when I hear an unfamiliar voice. Clear, soft and polite.

"Sorry to bother you …" he says. "Um, I didn't catch your name earlier."

No, you didn't. Because I'm a moron incapable of holding a conversation.

"Sydney, sorry," I stutter turning around. I teeter on the top step, trying to lean casually against the railing on the wall.

"Sydney," he says with a ferociously handsome smile, "I'm Grant. Nice to meet you."

I nod. Still not functioning properly.

"Anyway, you wouldn't happen to know where Economics with Mr Palmatier would be, would you? The room number is missing from my schedule." He holds up the crumpled piece of carbon paper as evidence and flashes *the* smile again.

"Um, yeah," I stammer, heat filling my face. "That's actually where I'm headed. I could show you, if you'd like." My voice sounds foreign in my own ears. It's several octaves higher than normal from my stupid nerves.

"That'd be great. Thanks."

"Sure thing," I say.

I start to take a step, but haven't correctly gauged how close I am to the edge of the stairs. As if in slow motion, I lose my balance and fall down the short flight of steps and on to my back. *For the second time today.* My head hits the floor with a loud smack and I squeeze my eyes tightly together, hoping to stop the tears of humiliation and pain from forming. And maybe if I'm really lucky, Grant will miraculously disappear too. I think I liked the camera crew in my face better.

After what feels like ten minutes, although it's probably more like thirty seconds, I crack one eye open. Through my damp lashes, I see Grant hovering over me, hand outstretched. I wait for the laughter, or at least a smirk, but he fights it off. His brow is puckered and his face holds only a look of genuine concern. I'd almost rather he laugh than pity me. I'd had enough of that to last a lifetime.

"Let me help," he says, pulling me up off of the ground and dusting off the back of my jumper.

This is so far beyond mortifying. I have perfect balance. I can manage to stay on a four-inch-wide balance beam, four feet off of the ground, while flipping multiple times and somehow, in Grant's presence, I can't even keep upright standing still on a step more than twice its size?

"Are you okay?" he asks. There still isn't any amusement in his tone.

"Fine," I say, refusing to actually look at him. I brush the tears out of my eyes before he can see them, and fight the urge to rub the back of my pounding head. I feel stupid enough as it is, I'm not going to admit injury as well. I'm not sure why he's making me so nervous, but I need to get away.

I'm glad the cameras aren't here to see me rush off to Econ, leaving Grant to find his own way.

Three

My younger sister, Maisy, is sitting at the kitchen counter when I get home from gym that evening. She has a faraway look in her eyes, like something's bothering her.

"What's the matter?" I ask.

She doesn't answer. This is our typical exchange. I try to talk to her. She ignores me in favour of our cat. Or a magazine. Or a donut. It doesn't matter. Anything to avoid communicating with me.

"Hey, it's supposed to be beautiful this weekend. I was thinking you might want to do something together? Anywhere you want to go?" I press. I'm trying. I really am. I try to remind myself that Maisy was young when mom died. That she didn't have the same childhood I did. That she might be even more lost than I am.

"Nope. I have plans," she says without looking up.

Of course she does, the little social butterfly.

"Okay. Well, let me know if plans change," I say.

I'm relieved when Dad comes home with bags of take-out and interrupts the uncomfortable silence in the house.

My dad, Everett Pierce, is an architect. Designing buildings is the reason for his existence. At least since my mom died. They were high school sweethearts. And I know that sounds totally lame and generic, but in their case, it was really sweet. He's a good looking guy, even though he looks tired tonight – in fact he looks tired a lot of the time now. I think, like me, he's still having trouble getting a good night's rest. His hair has just the right amount of grey to keep him looking handsome and distinguished, rather than over the hill. I worry sometimes that his loyalty to my mom will keep him from being happy with someone else. I guess only time will tell.

I pick out some brown rice and Mandarin chicken from the takeout bags and head up to my room to start my homework. There's only so many awkward silences that I can stand.My palm clutches my chest in an attempt to slow my pounding heart. My eyes struggle to focus on the alarm clock.

Blink. Blink. Blink.

4:45 A.M. slowly comes into focus.

Oh, well, I reason with myself. My alarm was going to go off in fifteen minutes anyhow. I fling the thick comforter off of the bed.

The nightmare that's just woken me up isn't a new one. I've had the same one so many times. Less frequently since Trevor and I have been together, but that doesn't mean that it stings any less. I suppose calling it a nightmare isn't even entirely accurate. Not when it's something that actually happened; the morning that changed my life is the stuff nightmares are made of. I was only fifteen when someone killed my mom.

Confessional

I can't go back to sleep, so I might as well be doing this. I smooth the jumper that I'd thrown on, making sure it covers up my pajama shirt. The camera is positioned to only capture me from the waist up, so I didn't bother changing out of my pajama bottoms. "I'm up early for my workout this morning. I just couldn't sleep because I'm so excited to get to gym and start working on my routines for Nationals." I wish these nightmares would stop. She's gone. I get it. I don't understand why my brain insists on making me relive it night after night. I fight a yawn coming on. "To be honest—" I miss my mom. I wish she were here to help me figure out this crazy schedule, this crazy show, this crazy life. But I can't say any of that, no matter how true it is. "To be honest, there's nothing I'd rather do than gymnastics. There's nothing that makes me happier than learning a new skill and doing it well." The tears I felt threatening to spill are kept at bay. For now. "So, I'd better get going!"

Four

Sitting in first period today is the same as every other day. Organise books. Tap pencil. Stare off into space thinking about Trevor. Or gymnastics. What the heck am I supposed to talk about in my "confessional" today? My life is so dull.

Until the door opens and Grant walks into the room. I'd almost forgotten about my absurd reaction to him until right now, when I feel my stomach fill with nervous butterflies again.

Mrs Drez is already passing out instructions for a partnered assignment by the time he makes his way to our table and sets his backpack down. Grant picks up the paper to examine it before I can.

"Bathymetric charts, huh?" he says. I've heard about this project from upper classmen. Apparently, it's quite the undertaking.

I nod silently. Smooth, Syd.

Mrs Drez clears her throat. Like that will even do the slightest bit of good.

"Your partner will be the person sitting next to you." I glance over and Grant nods at me. *Grand.* "You'll need to work together outside of school to get all of this done. It's due next Wednesday. Have at it."

"Looks like we're partners," Grant says. I have to admit, I'm really glad that he seems to be way too nice to make any jokes about my nosedive yesterday.

15

"Yep. Can I see that?" Not having my paws on the instructions has me twitchy. I motion for the instruction sheet and he passes the page to me.

I quickly skim the directions and then glance back up at him. Same freakishly white, toothy smile. Same goose bumps covering my arms. Damn.

"This says that we have to meet outside of school—"

"I'm free anytime. How about you?" he says.

"Actually, I'm fairly busy," I say. Which sounds all wrong but Grant doesn't give me a chance to explain how hectic my schedule is at the moment..

"Oh, okay. Well, I can just do the project if that'd be easier for you," Grant says and shifts his body away from me slightly. It surprises me how much I don't like that.

"No, that's not what I meant. I just have a lot going on. I can't do right after school or anything, but I can meet up in the evenings if that's okay with you."

He smiles warmly at me. "Yep, evenings are fine. How about tonight?"

All right, Mr Eager.

I think for a minute about what I may have going on. Just one thing. As usual.

"Tonight works. I have gym until six, then I'm free," I tell him.

"Gym?"

"Yeah," I catch myself twirling my hair around my finger like a total dimwit. "I do gymnastics."

"No kidding. Not at the place out on Parker Lane?" he asks.

"Yep, Sam's Gymnastics Academy. I've been going since I was three." I can't tell if that sounds impressive or really lame.

"That's right around the corner from my house. I've noticed it on my way to school. You could just come over to my place when

16

you're done if you'd like, since you'll be practically there already," he offers.

That makes sense and also means the whole, 'going to a strange guy's house after dark' thing a little less weird since he lives in a familiar area.

"That's great. I'll be by about six-thirty. Can I bring anything?"

"I'll take care of everything."

Grant scribbles something on to a piece of paper and slides it towards me. I glance down at his address and phone number. The chart will be too cumbersome and have too many little pieces while it's being assembled to be stored at school, or carted back and forth to class. I get it, but I still hate when teachers assign projects that we have to do them outside of school. I guess hanging with Grant does make it a little more enticing. The project is not exactly complicated, just tedious. Basically, we have to assemble a map of the ocean floor, building it up to scale using layers of paper. I'm clueless as to how this will be useful at any point in my life, then again, Oceanography isn't exactly my dream class. I'm taking it because my dad mentioned how much he loved the class when he was young, so of course I signed up.

"See you tonight then," he says. The confidence in his voice matches his smile, and I inappropriately swoon a little bit inside.

The lunch room is noisy and crowded as always. Even more so today because a camera guy from the show is here filming some test shots, so even the kids that don't typically eat on campus are here, wanting their chance to be on TV. I set my lunch down across from one of my best friends, Tessa, and try to ignore the camera in the corner of the room. At least they aren't actually filming me today.

"Syd! I've been waiting to talk to you all day! Are we going dress shopping tonight, or what?" Tessa is beaming. I hate that I'm about to let her down.

17

"What? Did you finally ask Oliver?" I ask. Tess had been struggling for weeks about whether or not she should ask Oliver, who she's had her eye on for ages, to prom.

"Yes! So, tonight?" Tessa's voice is pleading.

Quinn is the next to show up, plopping down next to Tessa.

"Shopping yes, but not tonight," I say.

Tessa's mouth puckers downward into an exaggerated frown.

I laugh, just as Trevor appears. He kisses the top of my head and then straddles the bench seat, wraps his arms around my waist, and pulls me in closer to him. I love how close he always wants me. Even if the cameras are around.

"Sorry, Tessa, I've got an Oceanography project I have to work on tonight. I'm all yours tomorrow, though," I explain.

"Oceanography? On a Friday night? Isn't that supposed to be, like, a cake class? Aquarium field trips and tide pools and all that?" Quinn asks while peering inside her lunch bag.

"Yeah, that'd be nice. We're making bathymetric charts," I say.

"Bath-a-who?" Quinn asks, pulling out several small Tupperware from her bag. No doubt she has whipped up some amazing culinary creation that will put my usual, plain boiled chicken breast to shame.

"It's a map of the ocean floor," I say with a laugh.

"You need help, baby? I still have most of my projects from when I took that class last year," Trevor offers.

"No thanks. You know I'm not a cheater," I joke. "Besides, it's a partnered project, it shouldn't be too much work," I say.

"Depends on who your partner is," Tessa pipes in. She, like me, usually ends up doing the majority of the work in any paired assignment. It's just makes it easier to ensure that things get done right and on time. I look up from my lunch and realise that everyone at the table is waiting on my answer.

"It's this new guy. Grant Evans," I answer as nonchalantly as possible.

Quinn snorts.

I'd assumed no one would know who I was talking about. Clearly I'd underestimated Quinn's hottie radar.

"Oh holy hell, I've seen him about, he's *gorgeous!*" she blurts out. "Let me know if you want me to take your place in Oceanography, Syd. Seriously. Everyone's talking about him. Sex-on-a-stick that one is. You can go to my Bio Two class. Take a crack at raising my grade." Quinn is laughing hysterically, and I'm sort of wishing it was possible to stab someone with just a look.

Trevor's eyes are on me, I can feel them. Like his tightening grasp on my hand, they show that he's not happy with Quinn's description of Grant.

"Gorgeous, huh?" he says. His tone is light, almost sarcastic. Clearly he isn't worried, right?

I fumble through my backpack – looking for ... nothing. "Yeah, I didn't actually notice that, but thanks for the offer, Quinn." I work to make my voice even and casual.

"I love that you're partners," Quinn continues to giggle through her words. "Isn't that, like, how you and Trevor hooked up?"

I shake my head at her with a pleading glance for her to shut up. We've been best friends for years, but right now, I'd love to pretend that I don't know her.

Trevor narrows his eyes in Quinn's direction. There's a mutual dislike between them that I can't get to the bottom of. It's hard when your best friend and your boyfriend don't like each other. There isn't ever a light banter with the three of us; it's always work. No double dates. No looking out for each other.

"So, anyway, are we not talking about the fact that there is a dude filming you over there, Syd?" Quinn asks. I can see how those reality stars tune the cameras out, it has only been a couple of days of them following me and I've already almost stopped noticing.

"We were trying not to," I say. "And he's not filming *me*, he's just testing the lighting and stuff in here."

Trevor pushes his tray away as if he has suddenly lost his appetite.

Sorry, Quinn mouths. She doesn't really look all that sorry.

"I thought you said that you turned that show down?" Trevor says through tight lips.

"No, I said that they'd probably turn *me* down," I say. "We've been over this, Trevor."

"Whatever," Trevor mumbles. I don't really understand how pretending we hadn't already had it out about this topic is helpful.

"Anyway, shopping tomorrow, gals?" Tessa the saint says, changing the subject. She pulls a stack of glossy magazines from her tote and slams them on to the table.

"That's my cue to leave!" Trevor smiles and kisses me quickly before heading to the other side of the table to sit with his friends.

"Thank you," I whisper to Tess relieved to not have to talk to Trevor about the show. Or Grant.

Five

I rush through my workout after school. Sam can tell that I'm just not focused, and asks me several times if I'm okay. I tell him that I am, of course. I'm not sure what is bothering me, or why I feel so uneasy. If it's that I still hadn't talked to my dad about prom, or that Grant keeps invading my thoughts, or that I'm worrying that things with me and Trevor are going to go downhill because of the documentary. It's all just a little too much.

I hadn't planned on doing anything after my post-school training session, so I don't have any extra clothes or my toiletry bag so I can freshen up before I head over to Grant's house. Instead I throw on a track suit over my leotard and try my best to smooth out my ponytail. After about five minutes of only succeeding in creating more lumps, I give up. Who am I trying to impress after all?

I head out of the gym, get into my car and drive towards Grant's house. He was right when he said that he lived near the gym, so it doesn't take me long to get to his road. As I drive down the street I can't help but gawk at the enormity of the homes. I knew the houses in this area were big, but this road is unbelievable. The homes are larger and larger the further down the street I go. I have to strain my eyes in the darkness to see the addresses in the dim light. The road curves slightly and I slow just in time to see the number 4429 on a mailbox at the end of a shell-covered driveway. This is it. It doesn't even look like there could be a house there. I turn cautiously down the dark driveway, imagining all sorts of ridiculous things along the lines of a Texas Chainsaw Massacre. I'm seriously considering turning back around. I don't know Grant from Adam, and really, it's just plain creepy back here. But just as my imagination has very nearly got the best of me, the road widens and reveals a sprawling, two-story brick estate home, surrounded by massive oak trees. Several lights are on in the house, making it look warm and inviting, despite its overwhelming size. The sense of dread in my stomach vanishes, but the nerves about seeing my lab partner are still there.

I park in the circular driveway and slowly walk up the large white steps of the house, careful not to fall like I did yesterday at school. When I reach the massive mahogany front door, I'm surprised by a petite woman, who opens the door to greet me before I can even knock. In all my anxiousness about working with Grant, I hadn't even taken into account meeting his parents.

Grant must get his height from his father because he's at least six foot two and this woman, his mom, I guess, is almost as short as I am. She's dressed casually in dark blue jeans and a black jumper, her shiny black hair, that also doesn't match Grant's light brown mess, is pulled back into a neat bun.

"Hi," I say awkwardly. "Um, Mrs Evans?"

She laughs lightly.

"Come on in," she says, holding the door wide open for me to walk through. "I'm not Mrs Evans, I'm Julie. You must be Sydney. Grant's expecting you, he's around here somewhere."

I follow her into the foyer. The house is sprawling. The ceilings are higher than any I have seen before. Even the oversized furniture appears dwarfed in this space. I'm grateful when I see Grant coming down the wide, winding staircase. He smiles and runs his hand through his thick, messy hair. He's dressed casually in a pair of worn-out blue jeans and a vintage-looking t-shirt. I notice that neither he nor Julie are wearing shoes. For a second, I contemplate kicking mine off as well.

"Hey, Sydney, come on in. Did you meet Jules?" he asks.

I nod and smile at Julie.

"She sort of runs things around here," Grant says.

"You two need anything before I head out for a bit?" Julie asks.

"I think we're good. Thanks," Grant says. Julie leaves through the front door, and I follow Grant into another part of the house.

"I thought that … never mind," I say.

"Jules was my mom? No. Although, she is here *more* than my mom," he says.

We stop in the kitchen. It's modern and full of granite and stainless steel, and really belongs in a home decorating magazine. Grant pauses on the opposite side of the kitchen island and looks at me from under a thick piece of hair. I fight the urge to push it out of his face. That's just weird, Syd.

"My mom travels a lot, so Jules takes care of everything. She's been with us since I was five. Anyway, I think I've got everything that we need here," he says. He finally pushes the stray hair back and I can't help but audibly sigh.

Grant has laid out a poster board to mount the map onto, and coloured paper to be carefully cut into thin strips. He's also found some cardboard and X-acto knives. We'll need to cut out pieces of cardboard to build up the different depths of the ocean floor and then put the coloured paper on top. By the time we're done, we'll have a scale map of the different depths of the ocean.

"Wow, you're way ahead of me, here," I say. I sort of feel like a jerk for not even thinking of any of this stuff.

"Well, I didn't have much to do after school. But you, you came straight from gym right? Are you hungry?"

I shake my head. "No, I'm fine, thanks."

He narrows his eyes at me as if he doesn't believe me.

"If you have a bottle of water that'd be great," I say.

"That, I do," he says and turns to the large stainless steel refrigerator and takes out a bottle of water and a large bowl of fruit.

"You know, just in case you get hungry," he says, setting both in front of me.

I really am starving; I just didn't want to be any trouble.

"So, you said you've been doing gymnastics since you were really little, huh?" Grant asks. He leans against the refrigerator with his arms casually crossed over his sturdy-looking chest.

"Yep, about thirteen years now," I say. I'm not exactly comfortable talking about myself. Which is super convenient since I'm getting paid to do it for this documentary.

"Impressive," he says.

I reach over and pull a green grape from its stem. Grant gives a little smirk that screams satisfaction as he watches me delve into the bowl of fresh fruit.

"What about you? What brought your family to Georgia?" I ask.

"Eh, nothing interesting," he says. "We move around a lot."

"What do your parents do? If you don't mind me asking?"

He shifts his weight, looking a little uncomfortable for the first time since I met him.

"My parents are separated. My dad is still in New York and mom is here with me ... sometimes. Like I said, she's rarely around." It's strange how Grant seems uncomfortable, but still speaks of their absence offhandedly.

"I'm sorry. That must be hard for you," I say.

He shrugs his shoulders. "Not really, I'm used to it. Plus, Jules is basically family and keeps things running ..."

"Well, that's good," I say, not really sure what else to add.

"So, what was up with the cameras filming you at lunch today?" he asks.

"Oh, that? You probably think I'm a total freak show. They were doing some test shots for this documentary I'm a part of."

"A documentary? Really? That sounds cool."

"Yeah, it's sort of following young, Olympic bound athletes. Kind of like a reality show, but it's only one programme. They want to see our real lives. Like I have anything interesting to show ..." I let my voice trail off.

"I'm sure you're fascinating." His dark green eyes don't leave mine as he talks and I can't help but brush my hand insecurely across my cheeks to ensure that I don't have anything on my face.

"Well, what about this chart?" I say, breaking his stare.

Grant and I are able to get a ton done on the project. All the while, holding a steady conversation. He's actually really easy to talk to. Not like when I first met Trevor and was so anxious around him that I couldn't hold a conversation. Something about Grant is warm. Comfortable. At school, I always feel like the girls, apart from Tessa and Quinn, avoid me. Like they're waiting for me to mess up so that they can swoop in on Trevor. Or that the teachers were waiting for me to crack under the pressure of school and gym and the loss of my mom. But with Grant, it's just ... easy. It's not like he expects anything from me, apart from what I am.

I can't stifle the deep yawn, just as the clock above the stove chimes eight, and I realise how long we've been working.

"Would you mind if we finished this up another day?" I ask.

"I see, trying to drop the ball, huh?" Grant says with a grin.

"No, nothing like that, I'm just exhausted."

"I'm kidding, Sydney. How about Monday. We could meet here after your workout again?"

25

"Sounds good." I grab my purse and head for the front door.

"I'll walk you to your car," Grant says, following me.

"You really don't have to do that, it's right on your drive," I laugh. "And this isn't exactly a dangerous neighbourhood."

"I don't mind." He shrugs.

We reach the door and Grant pulls it open for me, waiting for me to go ahead before following me down the steps. He waits until I'm in the car, with the ignition running before turning around and walks back to the gargantuan house with his hands in his jeans pockets. I know he said it doesn't bother him to be alone, but at that moment, I can't help but feel bad leaving him.

Even though it's Saturday, I still end up rushing around to get out the door to pick up Quinn and Tessa for our shopping trip.

I'd already been to the gym and back home to change. I really should have had plenty of time, but I find myself moving slowly. Dad is busy working in his office when I'm finally set to leave.

"See ya, Dad," I say, ducking my head into the doorway.

He barely glances up. Only pausing from his phone call for a split second to slide his AMEX to the edge of his drafting table and to tell me to be careful.

Maisy is on the sofa still in her pajamas, shovelling colourful cereal into her mouth and watching some ridiculous Guido-filled rerun on MTV.

"Morning, Maisy," I say. I playfully flick her in the back of the head. "It's gorgeous out today. I'm headed to the mall with Tess and Quinn, you want to come?"

She makes some sort of response that mostly sounds like a growl, and cereal drops out of her mouth back into her bowl. Cheerful as usual.

I'm celebrating the beautiful weather and an afternoon off by wearing a light baby blue sundress and white flip flops. I don't often wear shorts or dresses that show my legs. They're too freakishly toned to be exposed outside of the gym. Sometimes I wish I had long, slender legs like Maisy or the other girls at school. But my legs make me more powerful in gym and a lot of work has gone into getting those muscles.

I head out the house and towards my car. Pulling out into the road I start the route to Quinn's that's become like second nature to me. I pull up to her house, a traditional, large red brick home that screams perfect family from the outside, and send her a quick text message to let her know I'm here. Within a few seconds, both she and Tessa are bounding down the driveway.

"So, how was Grant?" Quinn asks before she even slides all the way into the passenger seat.

"Uh, good I guess. We're just working on a project, Quinn. Give it a rest," I say.

She smirks and starts scrolling through my iPod for something to listen to.

"Sure. But you have to admit, he is, like, beyond beautiful," she says.

"I'm not admitting anything."

Now, she's getting on my nerves.

"Oh, leave her alone, Quinn. You know she can't see anyone outside of Trevor," Tessa chimes in from the backseat.

"Whatever. You just wait till you see him, Tess. You. Will. Die," Quinn trills.

Thankfully, she finally settles on a song and turns the stereo up way too loud to be able to carry on a conversation.

The crowds at the mall always make me nervous. I'm too short to see around or above anyone. Quinn pulls both Tess and I into the first store we come to and starts flipping through racks of dresses.

Always the daring one, she quickly pulls out a floor length gown with heavy beading around the waist. The dress is mostly bright green and the material has the pattern of a peacock feather. The skirt of the gown is pleated chiffon and the criss-cross straps are heavily embellished.

I smirk. I wrongly assume she's joking.

"What? I'd totes wear this. It's awesome," Quinn says.

Tessa's taste is more similar to mine, meaning she's plain. We gravitate to basic black and pastels. Tess has what I consider to be the perfect shape. She used to be a little heavy, but now, she's all curves. She isn't lean like Quinn, or stumpy like me, she's just average. Average height. Average size. Sometimes, I wish I could be average *anything*. When Tess comes out of the dressing room with a baby blue gown with a plunging neckline and a Grecian look to it, I find myself fighting a moment of jealousy.

"It looks fabulous, Tess," I say. It really does. And it shows off her ample chest. Another drawback to being an elite gymnast – nothing going on up top.

"Yep, that's the one," Quinn agrees.

I look over and Quinn's wearing the flowing peacock dress. I have to give it to her, it isn't for me, but with her olive skin she looks great in it.

"Well?" Quinn asks.

"Perfect," Tess and I say together. Quinn jumps up and down, clapping enthusiastically.

They both head back into the changing rooms before taking the dresses to the cashier. Shopping has never been that easy for me. Everything I buy has to be altered to fit my small frame, and it makes trying things on difficult because it's hard to imagine what it will look like when it's 'fixed'. I feel guilty, but I drag Quinn and Tess to store after store searching for something that doesn't look ridiculous on me.

"You mind if we stop in here?" Tessa asks as we walk from the store out into the mall again. I glance up at the sign above the shop we're outside. It's a lingerie shop.

"Tess, you dirty, dirty girl," Quinn jokes.

"Shut up, Quinn. I need something to wear under this dress. Did you see the crazy neckline?" Tess says.

Quinn rolls her eyes and marches inside.

I find a bench near the fitting rooms to rest while I wait for the girls to browse. My neck aches. My head hurts. Actually, everything sort of hurts.

"Isn't this cute?" Quinn says, walking toward me with a tiny, black satin something or other.

"Uh, I guess? What's the occasion?" I ask.

"Not for me, for you!" she says.

I laugh and feel my prudish nerves kick in.

"Not exactly my thing, Quinn," I say. She knows good and well that I would never be caught dead in something like that. I sleep in pajama bottoms and a tank top, every single night.

Quinn clucks her tongue. "For the lake house."

"Oh!" The blush is definitely in full force now. "I don't think so. That's not me. Trevor knows that."

"Fine, but it's only your first time once," she says. "And it's not his, so …" She turns and crams the flimsy garment on to a full rack. She's right. It's going to be my first time. And I *do* want everything to be perfect. But there's no way I'm going to be any less nervous about everything if I'm strutting around in a black negligee. Even if it might be a welcome change for Trevor to see.

I wipe my nervous, sweaty palms on my dress. It's not like I'm going to be doing anything I don't want to do. Trevor and I have been together for a long time, and he hasn't forced the issue, but I'm clueless about what to expect. Up until now, we'd only had some

29

heated make-out sessions. He's always been patient with me, but he's about to graduate, and go away to college, and I know I want one of our last nights together to be the biggest of all.

"Okay, I'm ready," Tessa says, stepping out of the dressing room.

"Let's just call it a day, guys, I'm beat and we've been everywhere," I say after Tess has pays and we've left the store.

As the words are leaving my mouth, I see it.

The strapless, electric blue mini-dress that's meant for me in the window. The bubble hem is perfect for my height, and the frosted blue sequins that completely cover the dress are one of the most beautiful things I've ever seen. Best of all, it doesn't even need to be altered.

Six

The shopping trip must have gotten to me more than I'd originally thought. We didn't get in late, it was barely dark, but I immediately went upstairs and went to bed. I slept hard, all night long. Nightmare free.

I probably would have slept all day if I hadn't felt something lightly breezing across my face.

I try to open my eyes, but am blinded by the sunlight streaming in. Sunlight? I quickly shoot up in bed.

How long have I been sleeping?

What day is it?

Did I miss gym?

I hear a deep chuckle and turn to see Trevor sitting next to me on my bed.

"What in the world?" I ask. I blink repeatedly to ensure that I'm really awake.

"Good morning to you too, Sleeping Beauty," he says. It's more than a little strange to see him in my room. He's only made it past my dad and up here a couple of times.

"What time is it?" I grumble.

I love Trevor, but I have rules about talking when I first wake up. Like waiting an hour to swim after eating, I appreciate if no one speaks to me for the first thirty minutes that I'm awake.

"A little past noon," he says. "Your dad let me in on his way out. He's taking Maisy to Savannah for the day."

Nice. She told me she had plans this weekend, but didn't mention they were with Dad. Nice of her to invite me. Whatever.

"Oh," I say. "How long have you been here?"

He shrugs.

"Not long. A couple of hours. You were sleeping really hard," he says. He kisses me on the tip of my nose.

"You really should have woken me," I say, only half meaning it. Sunday is the only day that I don't have gym. I assume that's why Dad didn't wake me before he left. No one *ever* wakes me for anything on my one day off. Still, I feel guilty that Trevor has been sitting here waiting for me to wake up for hours. I stretch as far as I can in my bed. I feel my joints pop and for some reason, I feel unusually sore. I can't think of anything I did at gym this week to warrant the extra stiffness.

"Okay," I say, struggling to sit up. "I'm up, I'll get dressed, what do you want to do today?"

"Well," Trevor says, pushing me back down lightly with his index finger. "I think that's a bad idea." His smile is coy.

"What is?"

"You getting dressed," he says and reaches over to pull me in closer. His lips are hot on mine, and I love it, but no matter how good it feels, I can't let the thoughts of dental hygiene evaporate.

"Wait," I finally manage to pull away and gasp. "I need to brush my teeth, I'm disgusting."

"No you don't," he says, pulling me back toward him. God he smells good.

"Yeah, yeah I do. And besides, my dad could walk in any minute. We can't do this right now." I break free from his hold and stand up.

"He's hours away, Syd," Trevor says with a confident smile. "Now, why don't you come back to bed?" He reaches over and runs his hand up my thigh and I relent, letting him pull me back down on top of him. I'm stronger than most guys I know, but not Trevor. The way he kisses me is like physical proof that he wants nothing more than to be with me. It makes me tingle. It makes me unaware of everything going on apart from Trevor and me. Until his hand gently starts fumbling with the tie on my pajama pants, attempting to loosen them. I playfully swat his hand away and jump back up off of the bed.

"Oh come on, Syd," he groans. "You're killing me."

"You'll survive a little longer," I say with a light laugh. "I told you, we can't do this right now."

"Why?" he asks.

"The lake house."

"What difference does it make if it's here now or after prom?"

Good point.

But I'm just not ready at this exact moment. I still haven't even brushed my teeth. I want my first time to be special. Not spur of the moment because we happened to be alone. Plus, I need a little more time to get a handle on my nerves. I know I can't put him off much longer, though.

"Please. *Please* just try to be patient with me a little longer," I say.

"I've been really patient, Syd. You have to admit that. I just want to be with you. I don't see what the big deal it. Let me make love to you." His voice transforms into the most velvety smooth sound I've ever heard. His words tug at my heart, *and* my resolve.

I'm still standing beside the bed, staring down at him. His hand catches mine.

I take in his long, toned body. His thick blond hair that makes him look like he should be in a surfing magazine. That ridiculously handsome face. Any girl in the world would be lucky to have him. And somehow, he wants me. Just me.

33

"I'm sorry," I say softly "Please just give me a little more time." I push my lower lip out into the pouty way I know he can't resist and he lets out a loud sigh of concession and pulls himself upright.

"Fine," he says. He stands behind me and presses his lips to the back of my neck. "Can't blame me for trying, though."

"I love you," I whisper.

"Love you too, Syd."

When I wake up Monday morning, I feel like death. My head is pounding and the soreness from Sunday has only intensified. No good. My mom had always said that she wasn't 'allowed' to get sick. That's how I feel. I don't have time to be sick.

The cameras don't miss a single hideous second of me stumbling through my morning workout. They capture each and every fall, missed dismount and ugly toe point. I thought this show would be easy. That it would capture all of the good points, but right now, it feels like I'm being set up to fail. Finally, Sam takes pity on me and lets me leave thirty minutes early. As soon as I get home, I take a long, hot shower, and while the steam helps to clear the crud out of my head, it doesn't touch the achiness I feel all over my body. I would give anything to go back to bed, but that's not on the cards. Before I leave for school, I fumble through the medicine cabinet until I find a package of cold medicine and shove it into my backpack.

Trevor is waiting for me in our usual spot. As soon as he sees me, he starts in my direction and I'm immediately thankful for that small gesture so I don't have to trudge through the crowded quad. His face is full of confusion, and as I glance down, I quickly realise why. My tracksuit, combined with the messy bun on top of my head don't scream 'put together,' like my normal appearance.

"Nice of you to dress up, Syd," he says while pushing some stray hairs out of my eyes that I'd been too lazy to reach up and do for myself. "Jesus, you're burning up."

"I know," I sniffle. "I'm just waiting for this medicine to kick in. I'll be okay."

"Why don't you just go home? You can miss one day of school. The world won't end." He's right. One day won't kill me. Or anyone else for that matter. But it's just not in me to admit defeat and let a stupid case of the flu take over my day. If I'm going to take a day off, I want to be doing something fun. Not lying at home alone, sipping chicken broth.

"I'm really okay. Please don't make this a big deal."

"Text me if you need me to take you home early," he says as I walk into my first period class.

Grant is already seated when I slump into the chair next to him.

"Morning, Sydney," he says cheerfully. I cringe. He's too cheerful for the way I feel today.

"Morning," I grumble. I flop my head on to the table with a slight groan and wait for class to start. I can feel the pounding of my pulse in between my eyes. Miserable isn't even close to the word that describes how I feel.

"You don't look so hot," Grant says. "No offense," he quickly adds.

I halfway sit up. It's all I can manage.

"I'm good. Just a little cold."

"Why don't we reschedule you coming over tonight?"

"I'll be fine by then. Unless you'd rather me not come by and risk spreading my germs." I laugh. And then sneeze.

He narrows his eyes in a look of contemplation.

"If you're up for it, I'd love to have you," he says.

I pull up to Grant's house earlier than planned. Sam had all but kicked me out of the gym. The camera guy laughed out loud when

35

Sam told me that my 'snotting' all over the equipment didn't qualify as a workout. Strangely, I expected them to follow me to Grant's, and that I'd have to explain why they needed to watch us make a silly chart to him. But once I told them where I was headed, they backed off. Weird.

I wish I would have brought the piece of paper with Grant's phone number, I hate showing up early without calling first.

I take my time trudging up the large steps to Grant's house. They have either grown since the last time I was here, or my equilibrium is seriously off. Through the glass panel, I can see Julie making her way to the door.

"Hi, Sydney," Julie says. "Grant's upstairs, you can go on up."

"Thanks," I say. I'm about to ask which room is his, but she's already run off somewhere.

I slowly make my way up the staircase and down the long hallway. This is way out of my comfort zone. I pass several closed doors and then come to a half-open one. The room is dimly lit and there's faint music playing. The grey walls and sleek, modern furniture are a stark contrast to the antique formal furnishings in the rest of the house.

"Sydney?" Grant says. I nearly jump out of my skin at the sound of his voice. I spin around and he's right next to me. His thick hair is wet and dishevelled, and so help me, he is wearing nothing but a towel around his waist.

"Oh, gosh. Um. I'm so sorry. I should have called to say I'd be early. I just … um … Julie told me to come up, and …" I can't shut up. I try to avert my eyes from his chest. His abs.

He laughs and I officially feel like the dumbest person alive.

"It's fine. Come on in." He leads me into the grey room. *His room.* He picks up a stack of clothes off of the foot of his bed and heads out of the room. "Let me just throw these on."

I nod.

Because the sight of Grant.

Dripping.

In a towel.

Has left me speechless.

I survey the room while I wait. It's spotless. What teenage guy has a room this clean? One with a *chief of household-staff*, I reason. My mind flashes back to the sight of his well-toned abs and I immediately feel my face burn. *Stop it*, I scold myself. I pull out the desk chair and readjust my position repeatedly, trying not to look as self-conscious as I feel.

"Sorry about that," Grant says coming back. His hair is still damp and wild. And his jeans and fitted white t-shirt aren't making it any easier to fight the urge to ogle him.

"My fault," I say, waving my hand around nonchalantly.

"So, how are you feeling? Better?"

"Much better," I lie.

He narrows his eyes at me as if he's about to call me out on it, just as Julie knocks on the half-open door.

She's holding a small tray, which she quickly sets down at the end of the long birch desk that takes up the entire length of one side of the room and walks out.

"Thanks, Jules," Grant calls after her.

He stands up and grabs the back of the chair I'm sitting in and wheels me over to the side of the desk with the tray.

I stare up at him and his lips twitch upward in a small smirk.

"What's all this?" I ask.

"You aren't feeling any better, admit it," he says. "Try to eat something. Trust me, if anything can help, it's this. Jules makes the best chicken soup on the planet."

"Seriously? You had her do this for me?" I say.

"It's nothing," he says, waving me off. "Look, if it's cool we can just work up here. I'll run downstairs and get the stuff we started last week. You eat."

I do what I'm told and eat every last bite of the delicious home-made soup. Times like these make me miss my mom. She should be making me soup and taking care of me. Since she died, I've sort of been on my own in that regard. Sure Dad is physically there, but he's still hurting. Most days, he's just going through the motions.

"Good girl," Grant reappears and says, pointing towards the empty dish.

"Thank you for this. I really do feel a lot better now."

"Glad to hear it," he beams. "Here, relax while I set everything up." He's suddenly behind me, wrapping a warm, ivory-coloured blanket around my shoulders and leading me over to the small loveseat on the opposite side of the room. Being taken care of is a totally foreign feeling.

I pipe in with my two-cents sporadically, but mostly, Grant does the majority of the work while I lay under the plush quilt. I'm not typically this at ease in other peoples' homes, but things with Grant are easy. And I'm exhausted.

I remember closing my eyes for just a split second. But now, I'm cradled in someone's arms. I half crack my eyes to try to make sense of what's happening. Who's strong arms are these wrapped around me? Mmmm, who cares, I just want to stay like this. I finally open my eyes, and look up at Grant, carrying me down the winding staircase.

I frantically try to maneuver my way out of his grip.

"What's going on? I fell asleep?" I say.

"Shhh ..." he whispers. "I'm going to drive you home, Syd. You're exhausted." I start to wriggle again, but he grips me tighter.

"It's okay. I'm fine to drive," I say. I still fidget, but I'd be lying if I said I'm fighting as hard as I *should* be.

"Sydney, seriously. Not open for debate. I'll drive you home. Jules will follow in your car." His face is so close to mine, I can now see the short stubble on his chin and cheeks. The small cleft in his chin that I hadn't notice before. And the clean, soapy smell still lingers from his shower earlier. The way his arms feel around me is unreal. I give up my half-hearted attempt at a struggle and flop my head back down on to his chest. I know it's wrong. I know I should argue. But the truth is, I really don't feel up to driving home, and having someone take care of me feels flipping amazing. Especially someone that doesn't have to.

Grant effortlessly carries me through the house and out into the garage, then sets me down gently in the passenger seat of his car. The interior is impeccable, just like his room, and smells of rich leather. He starts the car and soft music that I don't recognise drifts me back to sleep.

Seven

I know immediately when I wake up that I've overslept for gym. And for the first time that I can remember, I just don't care. I'm still so tired. I wonder what Grant told my dad about bringing me home. I stumble over to my window overlooking the driveway and my car is parked in its usual place. I can't believe I slept that hard. How embarrassing. Oh, God, the show. I was supposed to do another segment this morning and I didn't even show up for gym. I pause at my door, not wanting to go downstairs and face the answering machine. There has to be a call from the producers wondering why I didn't show. There has to be. What am I going to tell them? They paid me to do this thing and I'm ruining it.

What if they show up here instead? What if instead of the staged confessionals, they start following me through my house with a crew? Exposing the one place that is mine, that I can focus on my own things. I can't let that happen. I have to do better from now on.

When I wander downstairs, I find the house deserted. The note on the counter from Dad says that he called Sam and the school – and the show. I'm off the hook for the day. *Wow.* I open the refrigerator and stare, uninterested at its contents. My stomach is grumbly, but nothing looks good, so I start back for the stairs.

I've almost made it to the top step when I hear a soft knock on the front door. Trevor, most likely. I haven't even checked my cell phone, but I'm willing to bet there are a dozen missed calls from him. I don't check the peep-hole and instead, fling the door open. But instead of Trevor, I find Grant standing on my porch, his messy brown hair blowing perfectly in the wind.

"Um, hi," I say. I pull my sleeves down over my hands and clutch them near my throat nervously. Each gust of wind blows his hair and makes my breath catch.

"Hey. Sorry to come by without calling. I just wanted to make sure you were all right. You were pretty worn out last night," he says.

"I'm doing okay," I say. "Thanks for bringing me home. I feel really stupid about everything."

I stare at a piece of chipped paint on the doorframe rather than make eye contact with him. Something that I've discovered is increasingly difficult, both because he always seems to be looking directly at me, but also, because I really *want* to look at him.

"Don't. I was happy to do it," he says.

Another gust of wind. Another chance to try to catch my breath.

"Do you want to come in?" I ask.

"I'd better get back to school. I just wanted to bring this by." He hands me a white paper bag with a small container inside.

My brows pull together in curiosity.

"It's some of Jules's soup," Grant explains. My stomach grumbles again, but this time in thanks. Nothing sounds better than more of this soup.

"Thank you!" I say. "Wow, you're pretty perfect, aren't you?" I can't help but gush before I have time to think about what I'm saying.

"Eh, I'm all right. You deserve it, though." He shoves his hands in his pockets, and before I know it, he's leaning in and kissing me lightly on my lips – just a peck – before he turns around and walks away. The spot where his warm lips touched mine is tingling with delight as I stand there half-dazed. Did that really just happen? In the same moment I'm contemplating whether or not I'm still actually asleep, I see the familiar Range Rover pull into the now vacant spot in the driveway. And that's when it dawns on me. Grant has no idea I have a boyfriend. Have I been leading him on?

I don't really have time to think much on it, because Trevor is walking up the drive. I quickly turn and set the bag on the counter, then plaster a big smile on my face. It's not phony. I *am* happy to see him. Just a little more conflicted than usual.

"Hey, beauty," Trevor says, wrapping his arms around my waist and leaning in to kiss me. I pull back abruptly.

"You don't want to do that, I'm really sick," I say, pulling farther away and covering my mouth.

"I don't care," he says, reaching for me again.

"Well, *I* do." I frown. I pull a bar stool out and sit down. My head feels like it's going to explode. I really do need to go back to bed.

"What are you doing out of school?" I ask, already anticipating the answer.

"What do you think?" he says. "You didn't reply to any of my texts or calls. I came to check on you."

"That's really sweet," I say. I rest my head on the cool marble counter top. It feels like anesthetic for my throbbing skull.

"So, since we're alone, what do you want to do?" Trevor asks with a wink.

"Don't even finish that thought. I'm so ill, Trevor, that's the last thing on my mind." I shake my head and swat him on the arm.

"You think maybe you should go to the doctor? You hear about those celebrities being treated for exhaustion. Maybe that's what's wrong with you."

"Maybe." I shrug. "After Nationals I'll have a break."

"Maybe you should think about dropping that reality show. You know, to give yourself a little break," he says.

"It's a documentary, not a reality show. And I can't. I signed a contract."

Trevor pushes a loud breath out.

"I love you," I add.

He starts rubbing my shoulders gently and I let myself relax and close my eyes.

"Hey, what's in the bag?" I open my eyes and he gestures to the white paper bag I'd tossed on to the counter. "Smells good."

"Oh, that? Just some soup. Want some?" I wrap my words in innocence before letting them escape my mouth. My heart has lodged itself into my throat. Why am I so nervous? It's just some totally innocent soup. Oh, yes, except for that mini-kiss from Grant.

"No, thanks. You should probably eat some though. Did your dad bring it by for you? You must really be laying it on thick, Syd, because he never takes a lunch, right?"

Why, today of all days is Trevor so ultra-observant?

"No, not Dad." I could tell him that Quinn made it. That's believable. She's always cooking something. But what if he'd already seen Quinn today at school? Would he know I was lying? Did I really need to lie? Would he even care if he knew Grant brought it to me? I take a deep breath. "Actually, my partner from Oceanography brought it by," I say harmlessly.

I stare at him, trying to gauge his reaction. His hand tightens on the back of the bar stool. His knuckles turn white from the stiffness of his grip and an unfamiliar flash of anger crosses his eyes. I've never really seen Trevor angry. Irritated, yes. Disappointed, sure. He isn't a gracious loser when it comes to his lacrosse games. He usually has a tough time dealing with it, holding the rage in and staying quiet for a long time. I never knew what to say in those moments, and I feel the same way right now. He's quiet. Motionless. For a long time.

"He came here?" he asks calmly, the sudden break from the silence startles me.

"Yeah, but just for a second. He didn't even come in. Just dropped it off," I say. It is the truth, but something in Trevor's eyes has me doubting that honesty is going to make a difference.

His eyes lock on mine. We don't have an intense relationship. This side of him is new.

"So, that was him leaving when I pulled up just now?" he asks. A sinister smirk fills his face.

"Yes," I nod.

In one quick movement, he spins the barstool I'm sitting in toward him, so that we are face to face, his fierce eyes boring into mine.

"What the hell is going on, Sydney?"

"What do you mean?" I ask. I jerk back away from his face. "I just told you."

"I mean, do you have feelings for this asshole, or what?"

"Are you joking?" I let out a nervous chuckle.

He continues to stare back at me. So, not joking.

"Trevor, there's nothing going on," I say firmly, cocking my head to the side. His penetrating stare is seriously starting to make me uncomfortable now. I straighten up and give him a quick kiss on his lips. Nothing. "No. No. No," I say. "Of *course* I don't have any feelings for him. Or anyone other than you. You know how much I love you."

He finally blinks and breaks the stare.

"Seriously." I pull Trevor's face back towards me, but apparently he's going to be stubborn, because now he's refusing to make eye contact with me at all.

He walks around to the other side of the kitchen.

44

"I'm sorry, Syd. But how would you feel if some girl was stopping by my house to bring me things?" His tone is filled with spite.

My head is pounding. I just want the argument to be over so that I can go to bed. Besides, Trevor does have a point. I'm more than a little insecure in our relationship already. I can't imagine if the situation were reversed.

"You're right," I concede. "I'm sorry. But please believe that it was completely innocent. Grant was just trying to be nice." I wonder if he can hear the bit of untruth in my voice.

"I understand," Trevor says. He takes the container out of the bag. "It's just that it's *my* job to take care of you. Not his." He walks to the sink, and before I can protest, he dumps the soup down the garbage disposal. "Do *you* understand, Sydney?"

His warm smile doesn't match his vengeful actions, so I just nod.

Eight

When I get to school the next morning, though I'm not feeling sick like yesterday, I can't shake the uneasiness. Trevor's lack of trust in me stung, but his anger was what really bothered me, it just seemed so out of character.

I park in my usual spot and pass Trevor's car on my way onto campus. I walk to the quad contemplating what I'll say to break the ice. Yesterday he left my house a few minutes after washing my lunch down the drain without saying much, and I can't help but feel nervous that I don't see him anywhere. He always waits for me in the quad before school. *Always.*

I stalk across campus alone towards Oceanography. While practising pirouettes on beam this morning, I resolved to tell Grant about Trevor. I mean, even though the kiss could have meant nothing, I feel awkward that I haven't been straightforward with him. So I decided I should tell him that I have a boyfriend, just in case he does feel *that way* about me. Not that he does.

I'm not entirely sure how I'm going to start this conversation. But it's the right thing. The mature thing. Right?

"There you are." I hear Trevor's voice behind me at the same time his muscular arms wrap around my waist. I spin towards him in confusion.

46

"There *I* am? *You* weren't waiting for me," I say.

He smiles apprehensively and kisses the tip of my nose.

"Yeah, sorry about that. I had something to take care of really quick. How are you feeling?"

"Much better." I'm still wondering what he's been up to, but decide against pressing him after our argument yesterday.

"Good. Don't want you sick and changing your mind about things," he says suggestively.

"Changing my mind about what 'things'?" I laugh.

"Oh, you know, with prom coming up, I just want to make sure you're feeling up to par," he says with a smirk.

"All right, all right," I say. I smack his shoulder. He doesn't even flinch. "Get your mind out of the gutter and get to class," I order.

He smiles broadly and then leans in and kisses me.

"Love you, Syd," he says.

"Love you too."

I watch Trevor walk away and then pause in the doorway to Oceanography. Grant is already at our table, with his head down and a book on his lap.

When I get to the table and set my things down, he doesn't look up. *Weird.* Yesterday he brings me soup, today, he isn't going to acknowledge I exist. Maybe he's just engrossed in his book? I take out my text book and binder and organise them on the table. He still hasn't acknowledged my presence.

"Morning," I say quietly. He doesn't respond.

"What are you reading?" I ask. I'm hoping to start some form of conversation so I can slip in, *FYI, I have a serious boyfriend.*

"Morning, Sydney," he says without glancing up. He flips his book closed, holding his place with his index finger to show me the cover.

"*Spoon River Anthology?*" I ask. "Any good?"

"Yep."

"What's it about?"

"The short version? It's about people's lives and their losses." His voice is uncharacteristically standoffish.

"Oh, well, maybe I'll give it a shot," I say. He nods and looks back down at his book. "Listen, Grant. I just wanted to thank you again for taking me home when I was sick."

He finally closes the book and turns toward me with a soft sigh. His lips curve into their typical, charming smile. But there's something else. Something more behind it. I can't tell if it's a good thing, or a bad thing.

"And I'll tell you again, Sydney, it was my pleasure. Anytime."

"Well, see, that's the thing," I say. I twist a lock of hair around my pencil nervously. "I don't know if I mentioned this before, but I, um, I have a boyfriend." I pause, waiting for him to respond.

"Nope, you didn't mention it," he says flatly. Crap. I'd been wrong. He *was* interested in me …

"Look, I'm really sorry for not mentioning it before—"

"Sydney, it's fine. I'm up for a little friendly competition," he says with a confident smile.

Chills run up my arms, my back and my neck. Did he really just say that?

"It won't be friendly," I mumble softly.

"I can handle it."

I can't.

I'm not sure what else to say. I glance up at him from under the protection of my hair, waiting for him to speak. He takes a deep breath as if he's thoughtfully weighing his words.

"Listen, Sydney. You didn't tell me that you were seeing someone. But your boyfriend, Trevor, I guess is his name, he did let me know."

My eyes bulge as Trevor's words from earlier run through my

48

mind: *I had something to take care of really quick.* He must have confronted Grant. I wipe my sweaty palms on my jeans.

"I'm so sorry," is all I can eke out.

Grant shrugs his shoulders coolly. "It's fine. Really. I'm sorry if I made you uncomfortable the other day."

"No. It's not that. I appreciate you bringing me home, and the soup and everything ... I just don't want you to think that I put him up to this," I say.

"I believe you. He said you had nothing to do with it."

"Really? What else did he say?" I ask. I want every single detail, but judging by Grant's cool demeanour, I'm not going to get much else.

"Not much. Just that he wanted to introduce himself and let me know that you two are exclusive. And that I shouldn't cross any boundaries. That's it." He really doesn't seem bothered by any of it.

"I don't know what to say."

"There's nothing to say, Sydney. I don't want to complicate your life, or your relationships. And honestly, you may get upset with me for saying this, but it seems to me that you deserve much better than him," Grant says. He flips his book back open, abruptly ending our conversation.

I immediately feel myself get defensive. Who the hell is he to say who and what I deserve? He barely knows me.

"Grant, that's not fair. You don't know anything."

He looks up from his book again and smiles. Toothy and cocky.

"I know that every time I'm around you I want to kiss you," he says matter-of-factly.

Heat fills my face. I've never been so glad to hear Mrs Drez's raspy throat clearing. If she hadn't interrupted, I would have had to leave class.

*

49

When I finally get to English later in the day, I can't wait to fill Quinn in on what happened.

"You're not going to believe this," I say.

Quinn smirks. "Uh-oh, what'd the douche-nozzle do this time?"

"Quinn, seriously, just listen."

She listens wide-eyed as I air my Trevor-Grant drama. Omitting the teeny-tiny kiss, so small, it isn't even worth mentioning. Or Grant's comment about wanting to do it again. My stomach flops remembering that detail of our conversation.

When I finish, Quinn smirks. "You should totally break up with Trevor and go for Grant!"

"Come on! I'm upset here!"

"I know you are. And I so wish that I had your problems!" she snickers. "But seriously, Syd. What the hell? Possessive much? Why did Trevor speak to Grant?"

I lean back in my chair and cross my arms over my chest.

"I don't know. It does bother me. But what bothers me even more is Grant's comment about me deserving better. Who does he think he is?" I slam my English book on my desk in frustration and everyone near me turns to stare.

"Well, Syd, I hate to say that I agree with him, but you know I do," she shrugs. Her lips twitch like she's fighting off a smile. I sort of dislike my best friend right now.

I know how she feels about Trevor, but she has no good reason for it, so I refuse to listen. He's never been anything but nice to her. Grant has just strolled right into my life and made a huge mess out of everything. From this second on, I refuse to let him do it any longer.

"Seriously, Quinn, give it a rest," I say. My tone nears callous. Quinn, her eyebrows raised in shock, shakes her head before turning to face forward.

I sigh and let my tense shoulders fall, feeling more than defeated. Not only has Grant caused an argument between me and Trevor, but he's sparked a fight with my best friend as well. Super.

Confessional

"This week has flown by. I have been training harder and harder in gym in preparation for Nationals." Thankfully, Trevor hasn't brought up the Grant situation at all, and I've been steering clear of it, too. "I finished up a major project at school, so that's a load off of me." Grant and I are barely speaking. There's nothing more than a brief exchange of words while passing worksheets to each other, or an "excuse me," if we accidently touch. I hate that things are so awkward, but it's really for the best. "And, right now, what I'm most excited about is that tonight is my Junior Prom! I've got everything packed up and ready to go to gym this morning, then I'll be headed over to my best friend's house to get ready. I can't wait to share the details of tonight with you guys!" That's a lie. I hope I can avoid the cameras and enjoy the night with Trevor and my friends. In peace. I never get to spend time with the people I care about anymore. Between school, gym, and Trevor, I'm lucky Quinn and Tessa haven't ditched me altogether. "I'll check in with you later and let you know how it all went!"

Nine

"Morning!" Dad calls from his office as I rush by the door. I quickly back up.

"Good morning!" I beam.

"You all set for tonight? Do you need anything?"

I shake my head. "I think I'm good."

"And you're still staying at Quinn's house after the dance?" he asks.

My heart is racing already. I made up the story about staying at Quinn's last week, but at least I finally told him something, right?

"Yep. A bunch of us."

"I'll be home if you need anything," he says. I smile at the sight of him tucking his drafting pencil behind his ear. I turn to walk away and he calls me back.

"Hey, Syd?"

I freeze, waiting for the interrogation.

"Be careful. And give me a call before you go to bed. Let me know you girls are safe, okay?" His concern touches me. And makes me feel like an even bigger jerk for lying.

"Sure, Dad." I nod.

"Love you, kiddo." He pulls the pencil out from behind his ear and looks back down at his blueprints.

I have to get out of here. My guilt is growing by the second. I grab my bag and dress and hurry out the door.

Despite my best efforts to persuade him otherwise, Sam isn't convinced that prom is a good enough excuse to miss my evening workout. I have to promise him that I'll come in tomorrow morning and work out alone to make up the time.

After gym I head to Tessa's only to find that Quinn is already there. Tessa's room is quickly a mess of makeup bags, dresses and shoes.

"So, is Grant going to be there tonight?" Quinn asks, swiping eyeliner along her eyelid expertly.

"I don't have a clue. We don't speak," is all I offer.

"Oh!" Tessa gasps. Her outburst almost causes me to stab myself in the eye with my mascara brush. "I finally saw him! Grant I mean," she says.

Her enthusiasm makes Quinn grin, and I roll my eyes.

"In my Library Science class," she continues. "He was returning a book. Something about spoons. Weird. Anyway, I noticed his name." She seems awfully pleased with herself for remembering the details of their minor encounter.

"And?" I say, trying unsuccessfully to mask my annoyance.

"Sorry, Syd. Quinn's right. He is super delicious."

Quinn chuckles. "Told you so."

"I don't mean anything by it, Sydney," Tess insists. "I was just saying that I saw him, and he's ... attractive."

I stare at my hands for a minute. Why are we even talking about Grant? Today is supposed to be about me and Trevor, I don't want to think about anyone else.

"Your eye makeup looks amazing, Quinn," I say softly. Unable to ignore the compliment of her skill, Quinn smiles and offers to do mine as well. Works like a charm.

"How is it possible that we're running late? We've been at this all day," Tess says looking at her watch.

We all dress as quickly as possible. Quinn is in her peacock dress with a green and gold necklace and large green ring. Tess's jewellery is more my speed. Simple. Tiny diamond studs dot her ears, and a thin diamond necklace is clasped around her neck. I want to ask if her jewellery is real, since her mom has recently "married-up", but I guess asking would be tacky.

My jewellery probably doesn't match my dress the best that it could, but there's no way I'd pass up a chance to wear it. A thin strand of freshwater pearls and matching bracelet. They had been my mothers. She and my dad had vacationed in Monterey, California for their anniversary a couple of months before she was killed, and Dad had bought them for her on the trip. The pearls are simple and beautiful, just like my mom was. I'd been waiting for a special occasion to wear them. I keep them locked up in my jewellery box; they're more valuable than any medal, of any colour, I've ever won.

"You look perfect," Tessa says sweetly, gesturing towards the pearls. I smile back at her, just as Quinn stomps her foot on the wood floor impatiently with her hand resting on her hip.

"Easy, Quinn, we're coming," Tessa says.

Tess's mom floats by excitedly as we hurry down the stairs.

"Come on! The boys are outside!" she says, grabbing her camera off the mantel. My stomach twists. This is it. I take a long, deep breath. This is the night I will always remember. The biggest night of my life so far.

Tessa's family has a beautiful home. The back deck overlooks a large pond, the perfect backdrop for our photos.

I smile when I see Trevor with Quinn's date, Daniel, and Tessa's date, Oliver, near the water. I feel a little guilty that Trevor is here with all of my friends, rather than with his before his own senior prom. We had compromised though – we'd meet here with my friends, since all of his would be at the lake house afterwards.

For once I'm able to sneak up behind Trevor. I playfully grab his sides and he turns around, with a big, cheesy grin plastered across his face. He picks me up and whirls me around effortlessly. I feel like a giddy kid.

"You are stunning," he says. He nuzzles his nose into the nape of my neck and holds me at eye level in his sturdy arms.

"You don't look so bad yourself," I murmur. I see the effect I have on him when the skin on his neck is covered in goose bumps. I never realised that I could make him nervous, too. I hear Tessa's mom shouting directions of where to stand, and how to pose for the photos, but I ignore her and kiss Trevor instead.

"Seriously, guys, quit so Tess's mom will shut up," Quinn says.

"All right," Trevor says. He kisses me lightly once more, then sets me down.

The photo shoot seems to go on forever before, thankfully, Tess's mom's camera battery dies. She tells us all to wait for her backup battery, but Tess finally convinces her that she's got enough shots so we can leave.

Tess and Quinn are going in one car with their dates and I'm going with Trevor in his Range Rover. He tosses my overnight bag in the back and we're on our way. Prom is being held at an historic theatre in downtown Atlanta. The theme is "A Night on the Nile". Mostly because the event was being held in the Egyptian ballroom of the restored theatre, and our prom committee was less than creative. I hadn't been to the theatre since my mom took Maisy and me to see The Nutcracker about five years ago.

Trevor reaches over and takes my hand with his free hand, while the other rests on the bottom of the steering wheel.

"You really do look beautiful," he says, kissing the top of each of my knuckles. "Are you ready?" he asks as we pull into the parking lot.

"Totally ready."

Ten

People are spilling out on to the street outside the theatre, waiting to get inside

"Nervous?" Trevor asks as we make our way through the crowd.

"Nope. Not at all," I lie. I look up to see if he buys my faux confidence, but he's already surveying the room, looking for his friends.

The inside of the theatre is phenomenal. I guess I'd half-expected to see crepe paper and balloons, but, instead, the formal room overwhelms me. It looks like it was decorated for a real ball or a black tie wedding, not some high school kids' dance. There's a grand marble stairway, trays of elegant finger foods, and most of my classmates are unrecognisable in their formal wear.

Trevor leads me to the dance floor, and my nerves return. I'm not that great of a dancer. I'm better at precise, choreographed movements, like in gymnastics, rather than things that require actual rhythm. Luckily, there are a few slow songs that I can manage. When the loud, thumping bass returns, I start to pull away.

"I'm going to see if I can find Quinn and Tess." Trevor nods with a grin. He's such a good sport.

"That's fine," he says. The cheesy smile hasn't left his face all night. I can't even imagine what it will look like in the morning.

"What?" I ask.

"Nothing. I'm just happy. Go. Find your friends. I'll be here when you're done," he says. Two of his lacrosse team mates arrive at his side and I leave him to catch up with them.

I survey the room looking for Quinn or Tess, but the crowd is too thick for me to see anything, even taking into account the high heels making me almost the height of a normal human being. I don't know if it's claustrophobia from the sea of people, or the fact that I haven't really eaten today, but I start to feel shaky and weak. I make my way to the food tables and grab a piece of chocolate-covered honeydew melon. I glance across the table for something salty to pair with the sweet melon. The tasty looking crostinis remind me of something that Quinn made a while back and I reach for one, just as someone else reaches for the same.

"Sorry," I say. I jerk my hand back.

"It's all yours." It's Grant. Looking nothing short of dashing. His messy hair is slightly more tame than usual, but not by much. He isn't wearing a tux like every other guy here. Instead, he's dressed in a simple grey suit and thick black tie.

"Oh," I say. I'm suddenly flustered.

"Sydney," he greets me with a nod.

"Thanks," I say, picking up the tiny piece of bread he just sacrificed.

"Don't mention it. You look nice."

I glance around the room, trying to place Trevor in the crowd, hoping to myself that he has his back to me somewhere.

"Thanks. Who are you here with?" I ask.

"Shayna Gillan," he says. Of course. Shayna Gillan, the quintessential high school girl that has it all. She's obnoxiously beautiful, wealthy, on every committee imaginable. And, *naturally*, a cheerleader. I'm actually surprised she's here with Grant, only because she typically only dates older guys. I guess if you were to make an exception to your rule, though, Grant would be worth it. I mentally scold myself for thinking about him like that.

"Huh," I mutter.

"She asked, and I didn't want to be rude," he says, shrugging his shoulders.

"Of course not. Well, have a good time," I say, turning slowly away from him.

"Sydney," he calls after me.

I spin around, wondering what on earth there is possibly left to say between us.

"If I had my choice, I'd be here with someone else tonight."

I feel my cheeks fill with colour, and I just stand there speechless. He looks totally sincere, his deep eyes gazing at me thoughtfully. Hadn't we already been over this, though?

I'm so dazed, Shayna manages to appear out of nowhere, linking her overly tan arm through Grant's and clutching him close. I can't be sure, but I swear he winced away from her touch. Shayna looks stunning. Her long, blonde hair flows into perfect curls down her back, and her dress is way too sophisticated for a high school dance. It's gold and completely beaded, and the front plunges so low, I'm surprised it successfully covered anything at all. I'm certain there's some sort of tape involved.

"There you are," Quinn says, walking up with Tess, both of their eyebrows peaked.

I nod. "Um, Grant, these are my best friends, Quinn and Tessa. And you guys both know Shayna."

"Nice to meet you both," Grant says politely.

Shayna is looking increasingly annoyed.

"Your dress is gorgeous," I say to her.

Her lips form a tight line. She's so damn unapproachable.

"It should be for what I paid for it. I had to have it made especially for me since I have a twenty-two inch waist, you know," she states smugly.

I will not roll my eyes. I will not roll my eyes. I will not roll my eyes.

Quinn scoffs. "Well, we can't all be blessed with an overactive gag reflex," she says.

I elbow her in the ribs, but it doesn't remove the smirk from her face.

"Quinn!" I snap, as Shayna squints her eyes at us and drags Grant away.

"What?" she asks, trying to sound innocent. She isn't a very good actress.

"So, what's going on with you and Grant?" Tessa asks.

"Nothing, we were just saying hello," I mutter and finally shove the crostini into my mouth.

"Is that allowed?" Quinn asks.

"Stop," I say, swallowing. "Are you guys having fun?" I ask, trying to change the subject. This is becoming a common practice.

"Not really," Quinn says. "Prom is pretty lame. I wish I was coming out to the lake house with the rest of you."

I tense up again, realising how close the big event is.

"How are you and Oliver getting along?" I ask Tess.

"Okay. He doesn't talk much, though. We danced a little. I just don't know if he's really into me," she says. I polish of the melon and throw my plate into the garbage. I look up and see Trevor headed our direction. The smile on his face leads me to believe he didn't see me talking to Grant, and I'm surprised at just how relieved I am.

"Hey you, wanna dance?" he asks, pulling me away from Quinn and Tessa.

We dance a few more songs. Every once in a while, I catch a glimpse of Grant and Shayna on the dance floor. They look like they're supposed to be together, and that makes me cringe a little.

Grant looks so at ease with a handsome smile on his face and his hand resting on her *twenty-two-inch-waist*. I can't stop my mind from wandering back to how safe I felt cradled in his arms the night I fell asleep at his house.

"Syd?" Trevor says. I shake my head, dissolving the thoughts of Grant. "Hey, lost ya there for a second."

"No way, I'm all yours," I say, smiling up at him.

"In that case, are you ready to get out of here?"

I look around the room, suddenly noticing how much it has cleared out.

"Sure, ready when you are. Just let me say goodbye to Quinn and Tess."

"Okay, I'll meet you out front," he says, kissing me on the cheek and breezing past me.

I find Quinn and Daniel dancing closely near an archway. I run over and whisper that I'm leaving.

"Good luck, be safe," she whispers back. Daniel smiles knowingly at me.

Nice, Quinn, way to keep your mouth shut.

Across the room, Tess and Oliver are sitting comfortably side-by-side. His arm is draped casually across her shoulders, and she's leaning into him, looking totally engrossed in their conversation. I turn back, glad that they've finally connected. I'll catch up with her tomorrow.

When I finally make it to the exit, my skin prickles with anticipation even in the warm, sticky Atlanta air. The streets are crowded, and Trevor and I sit in traffic for a long time before we're able to make our way to the interstate. I stare out the window up at the clear sky. The moon is massive tonight. I always feel so small when I really take the time to look at the moon, like I'm such a tiny speck in a massive universe. Tonight, it brightens the dark night in a peaceful way. I wonder if things that have always looked the same to me, like the moon, will somehow look different after tonight. Will I be the same Sydney when I wake up? I wonder if Trevor will look at me differently after we sleep together.

As we pull on to the ramp, I glance over at the car next to us. I jump a little in surprise as I see Grant and Shayna laughing together in his sleek, black car. I try to imagine what they're talking about. Is it a lighthearted chat like he and I had while we worked on our project? I imagine all of the interesting things that Shayna will have to add. Quickly I turn my attention back to Trevor and squeeze his free hand in mine. He speeds around the convertible in front of us, leaving Grant and Shayna far behind. Exactly where they belong tonight. On *our* night.

Eleven

The lake house is tucked deep back in the woods off of a narrow dirt road. I guess I'd sort of expected that Trevor and I would be the first ones to arrive, being that it's his family's house, but, surprisingly, when we pull down the drive, the place is packed.

I barely recognise any of the faces we pass as we make our way into the house. They're all Trevor's friends from our school, and some from his league lacrosse team. I can't help but feel a little out of place, even at his side. I really wish that Quinn or Tess were here.

After endless conversations in which I have zero participation in, the house starts to clear out. I'm standing in the doorway, watching the dozens of headlights disappear into the woods when Trevor comes up behind me. His touch signals a chill that starts at the top of my head and travels down through my toes. He brushes the hair off of the nape of my neck and presses his lips to it lightly.

"Well, hello there, stranger," I say, turning to face him. I wrap my arms around his neck.

"Hi, yourself," he says. He leans in and his lips part mine. Our mouths move together like this is their sole purpose. I'm completely lost in the moment, totally uncaring that there are still other people in the house. How did I get so lucky? How did I end up here tonight, with someone who loves me so completely? And then, I remember the lie I had to tell to be here. And my dad.

"Shoot!" I say, pulling away. Trevor grunts in frustration.

"What?" he asks, breathlessly.

"Just give me a minute, I forgot to call my dad," I say. Trevor rolls his eyes as I hold up a finger to signify one minute. I grab my iPhone off of the counter and make my way upstairs to find somewhere quiet to make my call.

Trevor's room is at the end of the hall. I've been here before with him and his parents during the summer. I close the door behind me and plop down on the enormous bed. I'm absolutely dreading making this call. I take a deep breath as I count the rings. One … Two … Three … *please go to voicemail, please go to voicemail*, I silently plead.

"Sydney?" Dad grumbles. Crap, I've woken him up.

"Hey, Dad, sorry to wake you. We're just headed to bed," I say quietly. I hold my breath waiting for his response.

"Okay, Syd. See you in the morning," he says in a groggy voice. My lungs thank me as I finally exhale.

"Okay, love you, Dad."

That was easier than I'd expected. I set my phone down on Trevor's desk and open the bedroom door. As I step out into the hall, I hear obnoxious giggling that can only belong to one person. It isn't the kind of laugh that makes you want to join in – it's the kind that annoys the crap out of you, especially in the dark, quiet house. I spin around, wide-eyed. Shayna and Grant stand at the end of the hall. What are they doing here? Why is Grant trying to ruin my night? Shayna's laughter is deafening and I can't even imagine anything in the world that could be that funny. Her back is pressed up against the wall and Grant is leaning in, trying to quiet her down. Talking softly. Too softly for me to hear. Damn. He leads her into one of the other bedrooms at the end of the hall, and closes the door behind them. I scowl at the closed door.

"Stupid rah-rah," I mumble under my breath.

I decide to wait for Trevor in his room instead, to avoid the risk of running into Grant and tip-toe back into his bedroom and quickly change out of this stupid dress and into my requisite pajama pants and tank-top and lay my pearls on his desk neatly. When Trevor finally finds me, my face is still hot with anger.

"What is Shayna Gillan doing here?" I demand. His head jerks back in surprise.

"Uh, I pretty much invited everyone, Syd. What's the problem?"

Grant having the nerve to show up here with her is the problem.

"Nothing," I sigh. "I just … I just didn't expect to see her here I guess."

"Okay," he mutters, shaking his head like I'm a crazy person. Which, obviously, I sort of am for worrying about Shayna and Grant right now. "Everything cool with your dad?"

He's changing the subject. He's probably chalked my mood up to being irked by his long ago confession that he once hooked up with Shayna. Then again, what guy within fifty miles hasn't?

"Yeah, I told him I was about to go to bed," I say.

That gets his attention. He lets the bag that he's holding fall to the ground and pulls me in close to him. His warm breath envelops my face, which surrounds me with familiarity, and anticipation of the new things that are about to happen.

"Well, then, I think that's exactly what we should do. Wouldn't want to lie to dear old Dad, would you?" he laughs.

The twisting nerves return to my stomach. His lips find the back of my neck again, his favourite spot, and then he pulls me down on to the bed with him.

"You're beautiful," he murmurs, cupping my face in his hands.

66

"I love you," I say.

He slides me closer to him, pressing himself against me. Every inch of me is shaky. And tingly. And perfect. The weight of him on top of me should feel crushing, but instead, it feels safe. It feels good to be so wanted. My hands fumble through his hair, down his strong arms. Trevor locks eyes with me as he pushes inside of me. Gently at first, and then thrusting deeper. I twist one fist into the sheet as my other hand fumbles over any bit of his skin I can touch. Anywhere. Everywhere. I just want to be closer. I try to concentrate on Trevor and how much I love him, rather than the pain that surprises me, even though it shouldn't. He moves slowly, trying not to hurt me. And for a while I let the closeness envelope me. But even being with Trevor, as perfect as it feels can't keep everything away. Tiny thoughts of Grant – down the hall – with Shayna claw at the edges of my thoughts and try to pull me away from this moment that I've waited for for so long. No.

No.

I'm here with Trevor now. Grant and that half-wit he's locked away with don't get to ruin this for me. My nails claw into his strong shoulders.

"Easy there, kitten," he rasps in my ear. "I'm not going anywhere." He pulls my earlobe into his mouth and nips at it with his front teeth.

This is where I belong.

My internal clock wakes me up the next morning when the room is still dark. I'm curled up next to Trevor, wearing his undershirt. I want to kick myself for promising Sam I'd workout this morning. I slide silently off of Trevor's warm chest and to the edge of the bed.

"Where do you think you're going?" he asks in a raspy, sleep filled voice. He reaches over and runs his fingers through my hair, tugging on it softly. A chill runs through me and I close my eyes, wishing more than I can remember wishing for anything before, that I could crawl back into bed with him.

"I have to go the gym," I say.

"I don't think so," Trevor says, pulling back down again and kissing my neck.

"I can't miss, I did yesterday."

"You worked out plenty last night," he says with a wink.

I frown at him. "You aren't making this easy."

His mouth finds the spot on my neck again. "Please stay. Who knows how long it'll be before I get to wake up next to you again?"

God I want to stay. I'd waited so long for this, and now I doubt it'll ever get old. I want to feel his arms around me again. I want to hold on to his strong bicep while he moves above me. I shake the thoughts from my head.

"I'm sorry. I have to go," I say, crawling towards him and kissing him lightly. He responds by biting on my bottom lip. He's so not making this easy.

"Come on, get up. I've got to get dressed and then you have to take me to my car."

Trevor sighs and flops back down onto his pillow. His annoyance with me is obvious, and after our phenomenal night, I'd be lying if I said it didn't sting.

I gather up my clothes and peek out the window at the rising sun over the lake. Outside, I hear a beep and glance towards the porch. My mouth involuntarily falls open. *Grant.* Wearing a white undershirt and his suit pants, and carrying Shayna in his arms to his car. Just like he cradled me at his house the other night. I push the anger away. I've just had the most incredible night of my life with Trevor. Who I love. Why should I care if Grant spent the night with Shayna?

I don't care.

Twelve

I unlock the door and flip on the lights inside the deserted gym. The familiar buzz of the overhead lights calms me and reminds me that I'm still the same Sydney I was yesterday.

Stretching on the springy mat feels good. I'm not only sore from missing yesterday's work-out, but from my *other* activities. I decide to work on floor exercise today since I'm alone. No equipment to fall off of, plus, Sam and I had added a new tumbling pass that I'm just getting used to for Nationals. I'm hoping to iron out some of the kinks and impress him in the morning.

I pound out one pass after another, until I'm about to drop from exhaustion. I decide to take a little break and grab my water bottle. It's near lunch time. I picture Quinn and Tessa still sleeping. Trevor probably drove back out to the lake house and passed back out after dropping me off at my car. I try to block the images from last night out long enough to get in a couple more tumbling runs.

"You made it!" Sam exclaims, startling me.

"Of course I did, I told you I would," I say. I wipe the sweat from my brow and smile.

"Pass looks great, kid. Good work," he says.

Sam and I have worked together for years. His demeanour is

usually nonchalant; he never gets overly excited about much that I do, even when I win – so making him proud feels amazing.

"So, you really came by to check up on me?" I ask.

"Not entirely. Your dad called."

My entire body stiffens. *Crappity crap crap crap.*

"The producers of the documentary called him last night. Did he tell you this yet?" Sam asks.

I shake my head.

"Okay, well, they're concerned about the material that you've been giving them."

I think back over the last couple of weeks. I have been slacking on my confessionals. I didn't do any spots while I was sick, and the ones I have done so far, have been more recaps of gym, leaving out anything personal. I know that's not what they were looking for.

"So, what does that mean?"

"It means that they're coming with us to Nationals. It means that they're going to be filming a lot more here. Also, your dad is supposed to talk to you about them filming social things. What's that boyfriend of yours name?"

The air leaves me.

"Trevor," I squeak.

"Yeah, have him take you out. Go out with Quinn. She should have plenty of time, it's not like she's ever here."

I nod. I can't say no. I'll finally be able to do something to help take the burden off of Dad with this documentary. But …

Trevor is going to freak.

Confessional

"I went to prom over the weekend. It was the first school dance I've ever been to. I went with a group of friends." *And my boyfriend, Trevor.* "It was amazing. I had such a great time." *I had sex for the first time.* "When I got home the next day, I watched a movie with Dad and Maisy." *I wished the entire time that I was back at Trevor's lake house with him. In bed.* "My workouts are running longer and longer in preparation for Nationals, but I think I finally have my tumbling pass near perfect. At least I hope so. I saw the list of names of the girls that I'll be competing against at Nationals, and it's a little nerve-wracking. I just hope to do well." *I'm the new girl to them; they have more experience than me. I have something to prove.*

Thirteen

"Morning, baby," Trevor says. I almost jog right past him on my way to first period, trying not to be late. I back up and kiss him quickly. "Did you oversleep?"

"No, I just lost track of time at gym. Then I had to get back home to make sure Maisy was up ..."

"You take on too much," he says, pulling me in as we walk together. I try to pick up the pace. I really don't want to be late, but Trevor is in no hurry. He's a senior and it's second semester. He's got all the time in the world.

"Not any more than usual, I guess."

"Maybe not. I just wish we could spend more time together," he says.

"We spend a lot of time together," I say.

"Not really. Not outside of school anymore. Think about it, when was the last time you let me take you to dinner?"

I shrug.

"It's just Nationals are coming up, and I've been swamped with homework ..."

"Okay. But will you let me take you out?"

I smile. I love this new attentiveness but when Trevor finds out about the cameras wanting to follow me around even more now ...

As quick as I think it, I replace the thought with the look of Dad's look of relief when I was picked for the show. Though he'd never said anything, I know what a big deal it is. How much it will help.

"Yes. Absolutely. We'll talk about it at lunch."

I slip into the door of Oceanography just as the second bell rings.

Grant glances up as I slide into my chair. As soon as I see his face, I remember my annoyance from Saturday night. I unpack my binder and book and don't give him the satisfaction of acknowledging him, but I can feel him staring at me.

Mrs Drez walks down the aisles passing out permission slips for a field trip to the Atlanta Aquarium. Quinn would be happy to know that her assessment of the class's activities was half true. Instead of sliding mine to me, Grant holds it hostage.

"Sydney?" he says, holding the paper to his chest.

He's going to freaking force me to have to look at him.

"What?" I ask, reaching for the permission slip. He doesn't hand it over.

"Did you have a good time Saturday night?" he asks politely.

"Did you?" I snap.

He doesn't seem affected by my sour tone.

"Eh," he says, shrugging his shoulders.

Oh, nice. You stay the night with the most beautiful girl in school and all she garners is an, eh? He's more arrogant than I had thought.

"I had an incredible time, actually," I say smugly.

"What'd you do after prom?" he asks.

I let out a loud laugh and Mrs Drez shoots a warning look my direction.

"What do you *think* I did?"

"Um, is this a trick question? I have no idea. I was just trying to make conversation," he says. Did he seriously not see me at the lake house? Was he really that oblivious when he was with Shayna? I

74

decide to give him the benefit of the doubt since he's never lied to me before.

"I went to my boyfriend's lake house. I saw you there, too," I say flatly.

He mulls this over for a second.

"That was your boyfriend's place?" His voice holds a twinge of amusement.

"Yep. And it sure seemed like you were enjoying yourself," I mumble. "Now, can I have my permission slip?"

"What?" he asks.

I shake my head without repeating myself. He looks puzzled as he processes the accusation.

"No, Sydney, it's not like that," he says. "I can totally explain."

"I'm sure you can," I say. I'm being absurd. I know it as the words come out, but I can't stop them. I have no right to be talking to him like this. I have a boyfriend, and Grant can spend time with whoever he wants. But Shayna? Of all people, Shayna?

"Sydney, just listen."

"You don't owe me any explantions, Grant. Really. Just answer this for me. Was spending time with Shayna to get back at me for not telling you about Trevor?"

He scoffs and I feel even more ridiculous.

"So, what, Trevor was the quid and Shayna was the *pro quo*? I don't think so, Syd. Playing games isn't my style."

He slides the permission slip across the table and positions his chair away from mine.

When I get to English, Quinn is practically foaming at the mouth for details about my night with Trevor. Her round of questioning is unending, but I tell her everything. Or, as much as I can without blushing. Or mentioning the fact that I saw Grant at the lake house.

She and I are so engrossed in our conversation, we don't notice Mr Brody standing right next to our desks. My face flushes as I wonder how much of our conversation he's heard, but Quinn just leans back in her chair casually and reaches up to pull her long brown hair back into a ponytail, as if she's clueless as to why he's standing here.

He sets a small, pink slip of paper on each of our desks and walks away with a grunt. Quinn rolls her eyes. Detention doesn't faze her, but to me, it's a different story. *I* have to go tell Sam that I'll have to miss another workout with Nationals around the corner.

When the bell rings, I tell Quinn to leave without me so that I can talk with Mr Brody. I plaster on my best guilty face.

"Yes, Miss Pierce?" he says curtly without looking up from his stack of papers. He's balding badly, but he tries to conceal that fact by parting his existing patch of hair in ways that it was never meant to be parted.

"I, um . . ." I stutter. I've never been in trouble at school before, so I don't know how to do this. "I'm so sorry for disrupting class, sir."

"And?" he says, briefly glancing up from his grading.

"And, I have gymnastics every day after school. I really can't miss. Is there a way that I could do, like, an extra assignment or something rather than detention?"

"No," he says categorically.

"Oh." My heart sinks.

"What I *will* do is schedule it for later in the week so that you can give adequate notice to whomever it is that you report to," he says.

I guess I could plan on working out extra this week to make up for what I'd miss later on. He hands me a new detention slip for Friday afternoon.

"Thank you," I say.

*

"So, did you get out of it?" Trevor asks sympathetically as I sit down at our lunch table. Quinn must have already spread the good word.

"No, he did reschedule it for Friday, though. I'm just going to have to work out extra this week to make up for what I'll miss," I sulk.

Trevor's mouth contorts into a grimace. I can feel the disappointment even before he speaks. Quinn and Tess must have clued into the sudden mood change, because they simultaneously get up to throw their lunch trays away.

"Friday?" he asks.

"Yes. I'm sorry, I know you wanted to do something that night, and we will. It'll just have to be after gym. And detention." I explain.

Trevor clasps his hands behind his head, sucks a quick breath in through his teeth. I hold mine. He's more than annoyed.

"I'm sorry," I repeat.

"You're right." He shakes off his annoyance, and I let out a relieved breath. "It's no big deal. Can I take you out tonight, then?"

"I think that can be arranged," I say, leaning in to him.

Right now, life can't get much better.

Detention aside, that is.

Confessional

I hit record and sit on the edge of the overstuffed chair. It's supposed to look plush and comfortable, but I feel the opposite of comfortable in front of this camera.

"I have to make this a quick bit tonight, because I have a date!" *I affix my best smile, though I'm cringing inside at having to reveal this part of my life.* "I'm so excited to be able to get out of the house and do something other than go to the gym, or work on school stuff." Grant and I turned in our Oceanography project this week. I should look at going out to dinner tonight as a celebration of that. No more complications. I hope. I tug nervously on the simple black linen maxi dress. "I'm not sure where my boyfriend and I are going, it's going to be a surprise, I think." *In reality, I just forgot to ask. I hope I'm dressed okay.* "I don't know if he'll be up for it, but I will try to get Trevor to come in and say hi to you all afterward!" *That's a lie. I have to tell him over dinner that this will be our last solo date before the cameras have to follow us. He'll likely go ballistic. I slip my gold flip flops back on and fix my lip gloss.*

Fourteen

Trevor and Dad are already talking sports, though I can't decipher which one. I can tell you everything you ever want to know about gymnastics, but that's my limit. I don't even understand lacrosse, and I've been to countless games to support Trevor.

"Are you ready?" I ask, stuffing my lip gloss and house key into my purse.

Trevor turns to me with a broad smile. "Yep. Nice talking with you, Sir," he says to Dad, shaking his hand.

"Was good to see you. You don't come around enough," Dad says to Trevor. "By the way, Syd, did you let the crew know where you're going?"

My heart lodges itself firmly in my throat. I cough. Or choke.

"Crew?" Trevor asks, raising his eyebrows.

"Yeah, I didn't, Dad, I was going to have one more night of freedom," I smile. Trevor is staring at me. Questioning me.

"The camera crew from the show wants to film a few spots of me doing something other than gymnastics," I explain to him.

"Cool, huh?" Dad says. He smoothes the pleats in his pants. "You kids be careful, don't be home late, Syd."

"Sure, Dad," I say, but my eyes don't dare leave Trevor's.

Dad leaves the room.

"We can talk about this in the car," Trevor says.

It isn't a long ride to the restaurant; it's just across town in Marietta Square. But the silence makes it feel like we should have crossed a state line. I don't typically come to the Square. It's normally pretty crowded and full of tourists, but even I can admit that the turn of the century vibe, thanks to the *Gone With the Wind* Movie Museum and other touristy hot spots, have made it a cute addition to our otherwise boring city.

We walk together past the unique shops that sell everything from eclectic and funky gifts to Asian antiques and sporting goods. With the sight of the restaurant, The Greek Tavern, my heart sinks a little. I'd secretly hoped that we'd go somewhere more on the casual side. But Trevor seems excited, and he hasn't brought up the show again, so, as usual, I put on my best enthusiastic smile as we're seated at a blue table with brightly lacquered red chairs. I eye the menu nervously. I have no clue what to order so I pick the first thing that I see that has the word chicken in it, figuring that's always a safe bet.

Once we're seated, Trevor reaches across the table and holds my hand and just stares. I let my eyes wander around the room uncomfortably, and then focus back on his, which haven't moved.

"What?" I finally ask him.

"Nothing at all, you just look beautiful."

"Right," I mumble. I'm so happy that the server arrives with our entrees and interrupts the awkwardness I'm feeling.

"Okay we have the Chicken Souvlaki for you, miss," he says, placing the plate in front of me. From the looks of the plate, I've made a good choice. "And the Paidakia for you, sir."

"My family and I are going out to the lake house for a week next month. Do you want to come with us?" Trevor asks in between bites.

"Oh! That reminds me, I left my pearls there, I have to get them back," I say, unintentionally ignoring his question.

"Okay. We can go and get them tonight."

"No, I can't. I told my dad I wouldn't be home late"

"Yeah, but wouldn't the extra alone time be well worth the trouble?" he asks suggestively.

I stare down at my skewered chicken to hide my flushed cheeks.

"Maybe some other time," I answer, hoping that he'll leave it at that.

"Right, because we'll get lots of chances when there's a camera crew following you. What about next month? Do you want to come with me and my family to the lake house?"

"I'm not sure. I'll have to wait and see how the dates match up with Nationals. And if my dad will even let me."

Trevor rolls his eyes in irritation, and that, in turn, annoys me. I can't help that my dad is different from his parents. They never have a problem with me going to Trevor's room, or closing the door. They've even offered to have me stay the night several times. I'm pretty sure that my dad assumes I've never even let Trevor see my bedroom. And as far as gymnastics is concerned, things will quiet down after Nationals. I can afford to take a breather after that, but I've worked way too hard to slack off now.

"I can't believe we're going to have to go out with cameras from here on out," he finally says. There it is.

"It's not going to be like that, Trevor. It's not every time. And I don't have a choice, they need more material. I signed on to do this—"

"Yeah, Syd, *you* signed on to do this, not me."

And he's right. I signed on to do this crazy thing, and expected him to just roll with it. It wasn't exactly fair of me to do that. I needed to do this to help with the cost of my training, but at what cost am I doing that? I never see my friends anymore, and my relationship with Trevor is suffering worse than I imagined. The rest of dinner is full of small talk, and I can feel Trevor's irritation with me silently growing.

When we walk to the car, I can't help but feel guilty for killing the mood of our supposed special evening. Once inside the car, Trevor leans over across the stiff leather seats. He cups my face in his hand and his thumb presses firmly into my chin.

"*I* love you," He says.

His tone sounds like a dare. Like he's trying to insinuate that I don't feel the same.

I nod.

"I love you too."

He holds my hand tightly the entire ride home.

Almost too tightly.

Almost.

Despite the awkwardness at the restaurant, the evening with Trevor had ended well and I was feeling so secure about us again, I had a little bounce in my step as I walked across the quad to meet up with him.

"Morning," I smile.

"Morning, gorgeous. You're in a good mood," Trevor says, draping his arm around my shoulders.

"Just happy I guess," I reach up and hold his hand that's resting on my shoulder.

"Do I make you happy?"

"*You* make me so much more than happy," I say. A couple of people scowl as they pass us in the hall.

"Hey, I meant to tell you, I have your necklace and stuff at my house."

"At your regular house?" I ask.

"Yeah, I drove out to the lake house last night to get it."

"Trevor! You didn't have to drive all the way out there to get my jewellery," I say, feeling guilty.

"I wanted to. I knew how important it is to you. I would've brought it to school, but I didn't want to risk anything happening to them."

"No, that's great. I'll stop by on my way home from gym tonight if that's okay?"

"Absolutely," he says. When he leans in and kisses me goodbye, I let my lips linger on his. I've kissed him hundreds of times before, but now, with everything about the show being out in the open and the fact we've taken things to the next level, somehow, I'd never felt closer to him than I do right now.

Mrs Drez is collecting permission slips for the aquarium trip when I walk into class. Grant is already in his chair, head down, and his nose in another book. His slip is already on the edge of the desk waiting to be collected. I take out my permission slip and hand it to Mrs Drez as she passes. When she picks up Grant's, he doesn't look up. For a moment, I debate whether or not to say something to break the ice with him, but I'm not sure what to say even if I had the nerve.

Mrs Drez makes another cycle around the class, passing out our grades for the bathymetric charts. She slides one down the smooth, black table towards Grant and me. We both reach for it simultaneously. I quickly withdraw my hand. Touching is off limits.

"Go ahead," I say quietly. He picks up the piece of paper and examines it, then hands it to me. I'm surprised to see that he's actually looking at me.

"Good job, partner," he says with a faint smile. I glance down at the sheet of paper. We got an A, naturally.

"You should be congratulating yourself, since you're the one who did all the work," I say, remembering how I lay comfortably on his sofa while he painstakingly assembled the complex chart. My thoughts drift to him carrying me down the long staircase and I shiver at the memory of his strong arms wrapped protectively around me. He narrows his eyes at me. Did he notice the small chill?

"I had a good time working with you, Sydney," he says carefully.

"You know, I enjoyed it, too," I say. It's honest. Albeit awkward.

We stare at each other silently for a moment, neither of us quite sure where the conversation should go from here. Mrs Drez finally makes her way back to the front of the classroom to announce that we need to pick up our charts after school if we want them, otherwise, they'll all be recycled. I really don't have any great desire to hang on to this project, but maybe it'll be helpful to Quinn next year if she decides to take Oceanography, or even Maisy down the line. Grant offers to meet me after school to help me get the large map to my car.

When I arrive at the classroom after school, Grant's already beaten me there and is leaning against the door frame, holding the large map easily under one arm.

"Lead the way," he says with a cheerful smile.

We walk to my car without talking much. But it isn't the same complicated silence of intentionally avoiding each other that has haunted us the last couple of weeks. Somehow, things have changed. Like both of us are just struggling to find the right words to break the ice. I, for one, am too nervous about saying the wrong thing to take a chance. Grant is the braver one, and speaks first.

"So, how's gymnastics going? I saw your name in the paper. You're going to a big competition?" he asks.

"That's right. Nationals are coming up," I say.

"That's really great, Sydney," he says. He flashes a genuine smile for the first time in a long time and his eyes light up like they did the night of prom.

"How about you?" I ask, hoping to continue the small-talk while turning the conversation away from me. "What's new in your world?"

"Same old stuff. I'm going out of town for a couple of days."

"Oh? Where to?" I ask. "Sorry, not my business." I bite my lip. *Way to overstep, Syd.*

"I'm headed to New York for a few days to see my brother and my dad."

"Wow. That sounds nice."

"You wanna come?" He asks with a smile. I can't tell whether or not he's joking, so I just smile and shrug. But something about his smile says, *'I dare you to say yes.'*

Grant loads the map into the trunk of my car and slams it shut. He runs his hand absently across the silver paint.

"Well, have a safe trip," I say.

"Thanks Sydney. See you in a few days." He turns away from me.

I'm not sure what possesses me to do what I do next. And even as I do it, I subconsciously know that I'll regret it. Grant has only made it a step or two away from me when I reach for his hand and pull him back towards me. His eyes smile with surprise.

"Thank you," I say. He stares back at me. Surely he knows that's not all I want to say. "I mean, thanks, for helping me get this to my car," I add. I drop his hand, and shove mine into the pockets of my jeans. I can't explain it. I just didn't want him to walk away yet.

"Not a problem," he says. He tilts his head slightly to one side curiously.

"It was nice to talk to you again. I've ..." I let my voice trail off, knowing that I'm only digging a bigger hole for myself.

"I've missed talking to you too, Sydney," Grant finishes for me.

I feel the heat on my cheeks and that's my cue to leave. As if there weren't a million before this.

"I'll see you in a few days," he says. He turns away from me again, and this time I keep my hands to myself and let him go. *What the hell was I thinking?*

I push myself too hard at gym, hoping to prolong the workout as long as possible. I want to stay in the protective, brightly coloured walls, where the outside world doesn't matter. All that matters in gym is how high I flip and how firmly I stick a landing. These are easy things in comparison to what's weighing on my heart and mind. I methodically analyze every movement in my floor routine, repeating each step over and over again in an attempt to perfect any possible flaw. Perfection. That's what I've always striven for. Finally, Sam forces me out, saying I'll be too sore to come back in the morning if I don't give it a rest for the night. I begrudgingly gather my things and drive to Trevor's house. I spend the drive trying to convince myself that I did nothing that I should feel guilty about. I was simply thanking Grant for staying after to help me to my car. I shouldn't be beating myself up over something so trivial.

Still, when I pull up to the modern two story home, I sit in my car for several minutes before getting up the nerve to walk up to the front door. Trevor answers wearing a pair of loose gym shorts and no shirt. Crappity. His parents are involved in a lot of social events in the community, and I don't have to ask to know that the dark house behind him means that they're out at some function. He holds my hand and leads me down to his bedroom, which is actually the converted basement. It's a far different feel from the sleek, Swedish style furnishings of Grant's bedroom, but really, why am I even comparing the two? Trevor's room is more what I think a typical teenage guy's room would look like. There's a pool table near one side and a large, dark brown leather sofa. The other side of the room houses a flat screen TV with an array of chords connecting countless video game consoles, and his floor is littered with clothes, books and video game controllers.

"Sorry about the mess," he says.

"It's fine," I say. I stare at the floor, not to inspect the clutter, but because I'm avoiding eye contact with him.

"You're in a weird mood, what's wrong?" he asks, taking my slight wrist into his large hand. When he kisses my knuckles, I feel relief course through me. Things are okay. I'm where I'm supposed to be.

"Nothing, just a long workout," I sigh. I hope I sound convincing. It *was* a long workout, that isn't a lie.

He sits down on the enormous bed and pulls me on to his lap. His hand presses into the back of my neck as he draws me in for a kiss. The force behind the movement is unusual. Heated and almost angry. His lips don't move with the same tenderness they had earlier today. He's kissing me like he has something to prove.

I finally pull away from his firm grasp, breathless and confused, and glance around the room awkwardly. *What the hell?* I spot my pearls on the edge of the nightstand and brush past Trevor to pick them up. I pause for a moment, letting myself admire them and feel a pang in my heart for my mom.

"Well, I'm beat. I'd better get going," I say, fumbling with the smooth pearls in my hands.

"Already?" He asks, stepping closer.

"Yeah, sorry, babe. I'm just worn out and I still have homework," I say.

I close the space between us and stand on my tiptoes to kiss him lightly, hoping that he'll let me go without a fight. I desperately want to shower and get to bed and have this day be over with.

But he doesn't kiss me back.

"Where were you this afternoon?" he asks. His entire presence has changed like someone's flipped a switch. Anger blazes across his normally calm face. He grabs at my wrists, not in the normal caress with which he usually touches me with.

"I told you. I was at gym," I say. I try to pull back, attempting to ease his crushing grip, but it only hurts worse.

"Really? Because I saw you with *him* after school," he spits.

It takes me a minute to process what he's actually accusing me of.

"Oh!" I say. "Grant? He was just helping me get our project to my car. Because I'm saving it. For Maisy." I'm rambling, and Trevor's grip hasn't relaxed on my now throbbing wrists. I turn them each way trying to pry myself free, but he doesn't seem to notice.

"Trevor, you're hurting me," I finally squeak out.

He still doesn't release me. It's not like the too-tight-hand-hold. It hurts. Plain and simple.

"I thought I made it clear that you were to stay away from him." The words seethe through his teeth.

"Trevor!" My anger and fear are both flaring. "We were just talking. Now seriously, let go of me."

I pull my hands back with all of my strength, sending the pearls flying in slow motion across the room before crashing to the ground, the necklace breaks instantly. I glare at him with hot tears quickly forming in my eyes. But there's nothing there. No apology. No look of remorse.

I scramble to the floor to pick up the still intact bracelet and a small handful of pearls that haven't rolled under the bed before turning back to him. He's finally stepped toward me with his arms extended. As if his holding me would somehow make things better.

"*You!* Stay away from me," I yell. I rub my sore wrists.

"Syd, I'm so damn sorry," he says, still reaching for me. The sight of his outstretched arms makes me queasy. Nothing about tonight makes any sense.

I grab my keys off of the bed and rush back up the stairs without saying a word. Trevor follows behind me, easily keeping pace as I hurry out the front door. I let it slam behind me, but he's back at my side as I fumble with my car keys at the driver's side door.

"Please talk to me. I'm so sorry," he says.

I open my car door the smallest possible crack and slip in, then lock the doors behind me. I don't glance up before backing out of the driveway and racing home.

Fifteen

I don't sleep well and am already up and dressed before my alarm goes off for gym. I'd spent the night tossing and turning, trying to make sense of Trevor's reaction. He'd obviously seen me touch Grant's hand. Was what he did to me my payback? Surely he didn't *mean* to hurt me like that, though. I'd never seen him so upset.

My wrists are achy, but I haven't turned a light on to inspect them yet. Mostly, I'm just devastated about the demise of Mom's pearls. How in the world could I let that happen to something so irreplaceable? Even if I could find some like them, I would never be able to forgive myself for ruining something so precious.

I beat Sam to the gym for once, so I'm able to have a few more minutes to myself. Once inside under the bright fluorescent lights, I'm horrified at the deep red bruises that decorate my wrists. I quickly fetch my wrist guards and grips from my gym bag and hurry to put them on before Sam comes in. I can't believe that I'm having to use guards that are meant to reduce the friction with the bar and minimise rips to my hands to conceal bruises. Bruises caused by Trevor. Thankfully, they camouflage them well without me having to add any extra athletic tape. If I did that, Sam would freak, worrying that I had some sort of injury. I can't afford that. I wince as I tighten the Velcro straps of the guards on my swollen wrists.

Sam comes in just as I'm prepping the bars with chalk.

"Good, we need to work on the Arabian double front today," he says.

I nod and do a kip to mount the low bar, cringing from the pain. And from his choice of skill.

I drive slowly to school. I've already been up for hours and am exhausted. I'm hoping to miss the first bell and make it to class with just enough time to not have to socialise at all. I'm glad it's raining lightly; everyone has taken refuge in their classes by the time I drive up. I grab a hooded jumper off of my backseat and pull it over my head, making sure it covers my hands and walk furtively to class like I'm a criminal.

I'm relieved to see Grant did in fact go out of town. I wonder what the likelihood of him deciding not to come back from New York is. I immediately feel guilty for even thinking that. It's not his fault that I'm so damn miserable. Still, Grant being away for a few days is probably good. Hopefully, his absence will at least prevent any more drama between me and Trevor.

The day drags on slowly. Quinn notices my foul mood in English, but doesn't pester me about it since we're both trying to avoid another round of detention slips.

By the time lunch rolls around, I've pretty much convinced myself that I overreacted. There's no way that Trevor meant to hurt me. It was just a stupid misunderstanding.

I set my tray down in my usual spot just as Trevor walks up. It's the first time I've seen him today and he looks uneasy. His hair is dishevelled, and his eyes look swollen and tired. His atypical appearance and the obvious reason behind it tug at my heart a bit.

"Hi," I mumble. Quinn's eyes dart up at my tone. No bubbly Sydney today.

"Can I talk to you, alone?" he asks.

Quinn puckers her brow, questioning me silently with her eyes. I sigh, and give her a slight smile to show that everything is okay, before following Trevor out of the crowded cafeteria.

He walks out into the deserted quad and sits on a damp cement bench. I fold my arms across my chest and stare at him blankly.

"So, talk," I say flatly. He reaches for my hand and I quickly jerk it back, even though a big part of me just wants to crawl up into his lap and make all of the bad go away.

"Sydney, god, I'm so sorry about last night. I don't know what got into me." His eyes are soft and pleading. I don't respond. I don't know how to.

"I am so, so sorry," he repeats. He looks down and shakes his head back and forth in apparent disgust with himself.

I stand there silently in the mist, replaying what had happened with Grant. I try to imagine the roles reversed. I imagine that I'd seen Trevor with some hot girl. Knowing the insecurity that I already feel on a daily basis in our relationship, I can't imagine the added insecurity of seeing him touch someone else. I cringe at the thought. How could I not have immediately seen the situation from his eyes? I uncross my arms and reach for his hand. He looks up at me like a sad little boy, and it crushes my heart.

"I'm sorry, too," I say. And I mean it. He pulls me down on to his lap and holds me tightly for a long time, until the mist turns into full-on rain and sends us running. And laughing. And together.

Sam doesn't find it odd when I'm ready with grips on to work on the uneven bars again after school. I wish for miraculously quick healing bruises. I'm not sure how many more workouts he will allow me to devote entirely to bars, or how many more Arabian Double Fronts my sanity will allow.

When I get home from gym, Dad is working in his office as usual. Maisy is at the bar in the kitchen working on homework. I grab a bottle of water from the refrigerator and sit down next to her.

"Hey Maze," I say.

She barely looks up.

"I was wondering what you wanted to do for your birthday?"

She closes her book and perks up. She doesn't want anything crazy, just a sleepover with her friends. I can handle that. It feels good to see her so animated, and really, just to have her talking to me for once. Like I'm doing something right. After we brainstorm, she skips out of the room and she finishes her homework with a rare smile.

I spread out my books on my bed and try my best to concentrate on my homework, but who am I kidding? The emotional drain from the last couple of days has left me barely functional. I lay back on my fluffy stack of down pillows and frown as I notice the cluster of pearls on my nightstand. I find a small drawstring bag in my jewellery box and scoop the loose pearls carefully into it. It's early, but I flip the light off on my way back to my bed.

"I'm sorry, Mom." I say under my breath.

I slide the books off of my bed, letting them hit the floor one by one with a loud *thunk*, and curl up under my thick duvet and let the tears take over.

Confessional

"I worked on beam today for the first time in a few days."

I'm finally able to work on beam again. My long sleeved leotard covers what's left of the bruises. They're less ugly now, but still a gross shade of yellowish-green.

"I'm able to do some of my best thinking up on beam."

Unless I'm working on a difficult skill, Sam doesn't hover.

"My pike double back dismount is pretty flawless. I stuck the landing perfectly today."

My feet slammed into the mat with such powerful force behind them, for a second I didn't feel so damn weak.

"This is what I've worked so hard for for so many years."

Sixteen

"So, what are we doing tonight?" Trevor asks as we walk to class after lunch on Friday.

"I have detention right after school," I moan. He snickers at my annoyance. And it's light. And happy. And normal.

"That's okay. Why don't I come by later tonight?" he suggests. He tilts my chin up with his thumb. "We can just watch a movie or something."

"That sounds perfect," I grin. Luckily, I've worked out so much this week, I'll be able to head straight home after detention and get comfortable while I wait for Trevor.

I stare out the window of the detention room, watching the rain and wind whip the trees around. What a miserable afternoon. I probably have some homework I could be working on, but instead, I spend the two hours dreaming of getting home and curling up on the couch with Trevor. It's been such a long week. I'm so glad that once I get out of here, it'll officially be over.

I hurry to my car after detention, not even attempting to avoid the puddles. My jeans have soaked up the water and are now saturated past my knees.

"Come on. Come on," I mumble under my breath, as my wet fingers slip on my car key. I finally get the door open and jump inside.

The warmth of my car envelops me. I catch a glimpse of myself in the rear view mirror. My long hair is plastered to the sides of my face and still dripping. I can't help but laugh out loud. I reach into the back seat and grab a towel out of my gym back and dab at my face and hair, trying to absorb some of the water as I look around the deserted school parking lot. There are only about a half a dozen cars left.

I toss the towel behind me and then turn the car key.

Nothing.

I try again.

Nothing.

Why is this even happening? All I want to do is get home and into a tracksuit. I silently curse myself for being a rule-follower and not bringing my cell phone to school.

I try unsuccessfully once more to start the Toyota before accepting defeat. I take the key out and sprint towards the front office. At least the major downpour has slacked off. I pull on the door. Locked. This has got to be a joke.

Just as I turn the corner, I run into someone full speed. Grant. He catches me in his arms before I slip on the wet concrete.

"Hey!" he says, cheerfully with a wide smile.

"Uh, hi," I respond, backing away from him. "What are you doing here?" My tone is more abrupt than necessary. I catch a glint of confusion in his eyes – most likely because I haven't seen him since the day of the fight with Trevor. The incident in the parking lot floods my mind. How innocent it felt at the time. How much trouble it ended up causing. As far as Grant knows, though, we'd ended things on a positive note.

"My flight was delayed and I just got in. I came by to drop off my History paper. What are you still doing here?"

"I had detention," I say. I look around the empty campus for someone – *anyone* – else that I can ask for help. "And my car won't start," I admit, looking at my feet.

"Why don't I take you home?" He offers immediately, just like I knew he would.

"Actually, that's okay. But do you have your phone? I can just call my dad."

"Sure, no problem," he says. He reaches into the front pocket of his button up shirt and then hands me his iPhone.

I dial my dad's cell phone number and listen to it ring. *And ring.* And cringe when his voicemail picks up. There's no answer on the house phone, either.

"No answer, anywhere," I say, handing the phone back to him. "Thank you though." I turn away from him to walk back to my car. Eventually, Dad will come looking for me, right?

"Sydney," I hear him laugh as he follows behind me. "Where are you going? Let me take you home."

When I look up at him, his face is so warm and selfless. Am I really going to turn him down and risk spending the night in the school parking lot waiting for someone to come and get me? *No.*

I look around the deserted campus one last time. "Are you sure?" I ask.

"Positive, you know it's not any trouble. Come on," he says, motioning to his car across the lot.

I slip into his dry car, and I'm so happy to be out of the cold rain I could squeal. I pull off my dripping jumper and stuff it into my backpack.

"So, how was your trip?" I ask. I should keep it short and sweet with Grant. I should have walked home rather than get in the car with him. *I know.* But still, I can't help it.

"It was all right. Dry," he says smiling.

I laugh.

"So, you were able to spend some time with your dad?"

"Yeah. And my brother. Actually, the main reason for the trip was a friend's birthday."

"Wow, that's some trip for a birthday party."

I'm likely being insanely nosy, but he doesn't seem to mind. Maybe.

"Yeah, it was, um ..." He runs his hand across his scruffy cheek and pauses for a moment, "It was actually my ex-girlfriend's birthday."

"Oh. Wow. You flew across the country for an ex's birthday?" I'm impressed. And that gnawing feeling in the pit of my stomach is something unfamiliar. It couldn't be *jealousy*. I have no right or reason to be jealous.

Grant laughs softly but doesn't respond at first. Have I over-stepped again?

"Actually, we ended on good terms," he starts. His voice is thoughtful, which is pretty much standard for Grant.

In reality, there's so little that I actually know about Grant. I don't like that. I want more. To know more, I mean. Grant pulls into my driveway, and I'm surprised that the house is dark. Where is every-one? I should thank him and get out of the car, but he looks as though he might finish his thought. I wring my hands nervously. Stay? Go?

"Jesus, Sydney," he gasps. My eyes drop in the direction he's look-ing. My hands. My wrists, more precisely. I slide them in between my knees to conceal the bruises, as if he hasn't already had an eyeful.

"What the hell happened to your arms?" he asks, reaching for one of them. His touch is soft and careful, but I still shrug out of his gentle grasp and reach for the door handle.

"Thanks for the ride," I say, trying to end the conversation before it goes any further.

"Seriously, what happened?" he demands, more firmly this time.

"I …" My mind races. I want to tell him the truth – that my boyfriend is insanely jealous of him. That he saw us in the parking lot together and got mad at me. I want to tell him that this is why I can't be sitting in his car right now. I want to beg him to stay away from me. But I say none of those things.

"Gymnasts get bruises, Grant. My grips were too tight and I've been training really hard …" I stutter off a litany of excuses.

He narrows his eyes at me, those gorgeous dark eyes full of equal parts doubt and concern. It's painfully obvious that he isn't buying it.

"Really, thank you," I say stepping out of the car. He continues to stare at me.

"Sydney …" He starts. He lets out a low breath. "If someone …" he lets his voice trail off again. His hands tightly grip the steering wheel as he stares straight out the windshield.

I shake my head at him and let out a little chuckle while flashing the most convincing smile that I can muster. I scramble out of the car, closing the door softly behind me and walk slowly up the driveway. I know he's watching me walk away. I wish he'd drive off and not worry, or even think about me again. I don't look back as I walk through the front door. I don't want to see the look of pity in his eyes again.

There's a note taped to the refrigerator. Dad and Maisy have gone to Atlanta to do some shopping. I run upstairs to shower and change before Trevor gets here. The water is hot and soothing. I let it wash over my clammy skin, warming me. Calming me. I throw on some jogging bottoms and a long sleeved t-shirt and dry my hair before pulling it back into a loose ponytail. Finally. I'm home and comfortable.

Seventeen

The knock at the door startles me. I've curled up on the couch and nodded off for what couldn't have been more than a few minutes, though it was long enough that the house is completely dark when I wake up. I jump up, dazed momentarily and rub my eyes until I realise what's going on. Trevor is waiting on the doorstep with a small bouquet of peonies, my favourite.

"For me?" I ask, beaming.

"Course," He says. He hands me the flowers and I pull the door open for him.

"Come in."

"Are we alone?" he asks, peering around me into the dark house.

"Looks that way," I say with an uncharacteristic flirty grin. I quickly do the math in my head to calculate how much time we have alone based on Friday night Atlanta traffic and what time Dad and Maisy must have left, before leading Trevor upstairs behind me. Trevor makes himself comfortable, sprawling out on my bed while I scan my playlists before choosing Damien Rice. I hurry across the room and into Trevor's extended arms. It's a risky move, not knowing exactly what time Dad will be home. But the overwhelming desire to be close to Trevor tonight outweighs the risk. I'm desperate to make the week we'd just had disappear. Trevor touches the hem of my t-shirt and starts to pull it up over my head. Rather than pushing his hand away, I shock him by helping. The warmth of his breath on my skin is electrifying

I guess because I know what to expect, I'm not so nervous. He kisses me, I kiss back. I let his hand be my guide, and it's sweet, almost a game. His fingers on my skin are soft and gentle, and he lets out a low groan when his fingers dip below my underwear and I move my hand into the waistband of his boxers.

"Touch it," he breathes, his mouth close to my ear, the weight of his body suddenly heavy on my chest.

"Okay." I ignore the way my voice wobbles and move my hand down. I touch him, but maybe it's not what he wanted, not quite right, because his hand is around my wrist suddenly and he's pressing harder, faster. He pulls back and his mouth is pulled tight. He's breathing hard, and I feel invisible under him. I feel like all the sweetness just got stomped out of this moment, and I feel stupid for not being able to please him and having him have to use my hand like the rest of me isn't even connected. "Trevor? Please, can we stop?"

"Stop what?" He's in a rhythm now, and when I let my hand go slack, he tightens his fingers on my wrist.

"This. I'm ... uh, it just feels ..." I can't force the words out. I don't know how to tell him. The first time it all went so smoothly. How do I do this?

"Sorry," he mutters, dropping my hand and yanking my underwear down my legs. "I just get so turned on with you. You make me lose my mind, Syd." His smile is sweet, and I feel a crush of relief. There he is again; there's the guy I love. He races his fingers up my leg and presses into me, a little fast and hard. I try to suck back the gasp of shock, but I'm not quick enough.

He misinterprets my pain. "Ready? Oh, you're so ready. You're so damn beautiful, Sydney." His lips are on my neck, pressing so hard on my cheeks and lips, I worry he's going to bruise me.

He pulls his hand back and presses into me, quick and rough, his grip tightening on my hips when I try to pull away. He leans his forehead hard on mine and pumps into me, his eyes shut, his teeth barred.

I stop wiggling, even though I'm not quite comfortable. He's whispering how good it feels, how much he loves me, and I hate that I can't be more into it. I want to love it the way I did the first time. I screw my eyes shut and wrap my arms around him, even though I don't like it. Because I love him. And I know that this is just a stage. Just like my muscles scream and ache when I'm learning a new move, my body isn't attuned to this yet. But it will be. And I'll like doing it as much as Trevor does. Right now, it's for him, but soon it will be for both of us, and I'm fine waiting on that.

Finally, he's done, and, even though I don't have the same glow I did after the first time, I feel satisfied

"I love you," he whispers as we hold each other afterward.

"Love you, too," I say.

"I'm so sorry about this week," he says. He traces a line from the middle of my forehead, down my nose and to my chin. I crinkle my nose every time he brushes his finger near my eyebrow, which makes him do it repeatedly.

"It's over," I reply.

"Well, it's not going to happen again. I love you so much."

"I know." I really don't want to talk about our fight anymore. "We'd better get dressed. I'm not sure what time Dad will be home." I sit up and nudge him, then fumble around the dark room for my clothes.

"Hey, Syd, I meant to ask you." He pauses to pull the v-neck over his head.

"Yeah?" I'm already dressed and waiting by the bedroom door.

"Where's your car?"

"My car?" I choke out. My stomach lodges itself into my throat.

"Yeah, it's not out front."

"Ugh, it wouldn't start after detention," I say unhappily.

"That sucks, you should have called me. I would've come to get you," he says. He follows me down the hall with his hands in my back pockets. With him this close, can he feel me trembling?

"I didn't have my phone, and I don't know your number by heart." I stop at the top of the stairs and look at him, weighing the options of telling him the truth or not. I hold my breath. I know the question that's coming next.

"So, how'd you get home?"

"It was a total conspiracy against me today." I try to joke. "There was no one left at school, it was all locked up. But Grant was there and he drove me home."

Trevor opens his mouth to respond, but I reach up with my small hand and cover his lips with my fingers. His eyes swirl with anger. Surely he's not going to let a stupid ride home ruin tonight.

"Before you get all worked up, he just drove me home. It was pouring rain and I was stranded. That's it," I say. I take my hand from his mouth and wink. "You should be glad someone was there to save poor little me." I try for sweet and flirty.

I fail.

He doesn't say a word. He just glares at me with the same livid eyes that he had that day in the kitchen when he'd found the soup Grant brought over. The flash of anger that I'd found so new and unrecognisable that morning has become familiar.

"You make me sick," he says flatly. He shakes his head in disappointment.

My mouth falls open in shock. *Did I hear him correctly?*

"Trevor! That's not fair. It was just a ride home," I say. I'd expected him to be upset, but really, what did he expect me to do in the situation?

"You little *slut*," he mutters under his breath. His lips curl around the harsh words. He pushes past me aggressively as he bounds down the stairs.

I follow. Not because I intended to. Or even because I want to. But because when he pushes past me, I lose my balance and tumble down the steps behind me. I wince at the pain as I somersault down the hard, oak stairs. My head strikes each one with a thud. I throw my arms out to try to stop myself, but it does no good. I continue to fall. Trevor doesn't stop to help when I finally land at the foot of the stairs. He turns for a split second to stare down at me with a wicked, sickened expression before walking out the front door. He slams it behind him without a word.

As the door closes, I pull my knees up to my chest and sob. My hair has fallen out of the ponytail holder and has mixed with tears, matting it to my face just as the rain had earlier. Did he really just walk out without even checking on me?

Everything aches. My head. My ribs. My arms. Even my face hurts. I can't remember a time when everything felt as out of control as it does right now. Not even after Mom died. That was out of my hands. There was nothing to do but grieve. Now. This. This is my own doing, and I feel completely helpless to stop it.

The first argument Trevor and I ever had was after we'd only been dating for a month or two, and Trevor had gone to a party with some of his lacrosse buddies. He and I had plans the following day to go into Atlanta. I waited the entire day for him to pick me up. He never showed, and he wasn't answering his phone.

When it started to get late in the day, I got panicky that something bad had happened to him. I remember pulling up to his house and being so relieved to see his Range Rover parked outside. At least he'd made it home. My relief was short lived though, and my insecurity took over. We were still new in our relationship and I was still unconvinced that he could actually like me. I was sure that he'd met someone else at the party and that was why he refused to answer his phone. I stood on his porch for a good ten minutes before I worked up the nerve to ring the bell. His mom let me in and she said that he'd been downstairs in his room all day long.

I felt like such a fool. Of course he'd met someone else. There was nothing special about me at all, and it was widely known that he could do so much better than me. My heart sank when she remarked at what a great mood he was in. He'd had a great night, and he didn't want to be bothered with me. I thought about walking out right then and there.

In retrospect, maybe I should have walked away. Cut my losses then. Instead, I stood outside the basement door and knocked lightly, barely a tap. I told myself that if he didn't open the door right away, I would turn and leave, saving myself the humiliation. But the door flew open and he stood in front of me beaming. I'd never seen him so cheerful.

"Hey gorgeous," he said. He wrapped his arms around me and pulled me in for a deep, intense kiss. I jerked away from him. Up until that point, the physical aspect of our relationship had been pretty limited, and I was mortified to think that his mom might be within line of sight.

He led me into the basement and closed the door behind me. Trevor pressed me up against the closed door and quickly found my mouth with his again. His hands wandered places on me that they hadn't been before then. I wasn't used to that type of affection. It left me a little out of my mind. I'd almost forgotten why I'd even come over in the first place. And obviously, he wasn't mad at me. I pulled away from him and he let out a low, sexy moan.

"Where were you? We had plans," I demanded, my head still foggy from his kisses.

"We did?" He looked genuinely confused.

"Uh, yeah, we did. We were supposed to go to Atlanta today. How could you not remember?" I asked. I watched him process this, looking like he was searching through his memory to try to find the one with our plans.

"Oh hell, Syd, I'm so sorry. I completely forgot." He frowned and his features turned boyish and apologetic. I would've forgiven anything then just by looking at his sheepish smile.

Did that level of forgiveness still apply after tonight?

He reached for me again and pulled me into his arms. Smothering me with warmth. And the smell of Trevor. A little bit of sweat and that same clean-smelling cologne he'd worn since I met him. His arms used to be my protective place. When I pulled back from him though, something was off. It was something about his eyes. They were wide like saucers. His pupils were tiny pinpricks of ink. They didn't look normal, for sure. I remembered what his mom had just said about his abnormally good mood. All of the little pieces started to click into place.

"Are you on drugs?" I demanded, cocking my head to the side. I was being completely serious, but he laughed loudly as if I was joking.

"You are! You're high, aren't you?" I said. He continued to chuckle until he looked at me. He saw the seriousness in my face turn to tears. I don't know why I started to cry. Maybe it was because he was keeping secrets from me. Maybe it was because he was laughing at me. Maybe because I felt like I was losing him. Hot tears streamed uncontrollably down my face. His smile faded, and he looked like he might cry as well. And I was responsible for it. Just like I was the reason for him being so upset tonight.

"Syd, I'm so sorry. I don't know what I was thinking." He put his face in his hands.

"What did you *do?*" I demanded. I tried to pull his hands away from his face so that I could look at him, but he wouldn't budge. He didn't answer immediately, so I repeated the question.

"It was just one line," he said

"One line? What were you doing, cocaine? Are you completely insane?!" I yelled louder than I probably should have with his parents in the house, but I didn't care. I stormed across the room and headed for the door.

He caught my arm and turned me back towards him. Not sternly like he had more recently, he was much gentler with me back then.

"Please don't leave. I'm so sorry. I swear it was a one-time thing," he said. The look on his face made me pity him. I didn't know how to react to this side of Trevor. I'd only seen the public Trevor that everyone else knew up until this point.

"I just can't believe you did that," I said. I didn't know what else to say. For the first time, I'd felt disappointed, let down by someone else.

He dropped to his knees in front of me. Despite my anger and disappointment, I knew he felt bad enough. I tried to pull him back up off of the carpet, but he wouldn't stand. Instead, he clutched my hands softly in his.

"Please don't hate me Sydney," he said

"I don't hate you. I'll never hate you. Just please get up." I couldn't understand why he did what he did, but I wasn't willing to lose him over one mistake.

He stood up slowly, almost unwillingly. His hands wrapped soothingly around the back of my neck.

"I'm so sorry. I won't let you down again," he said

"I know. I believe you." *And I did.*

He leaned towards me, his forehead rested on mine. He looked at me, like no one had ever done before, *really* looking at me. In to me.

"I love you so much, baby," he whispered.

I'm pretty sure that my heart stopped beating when he said those words. I'd never expected anything serious with Trevor. Honestly, I hadn't even really expected him to stick around as long as he had this far.

No one other than my family had ever said that to me before. And it was the most magnificent statement ever.

"I love you, too," I sighed.

I never told my friends about the fight. I didn't want them to think badly of Trevor. I wanted them to like him, and approve of him, and us. It felt like if I told, I was betraying what Trevor and I had – or could have. So I kept quiet. Just like I would do now.

That fight felt like the end of the world at the time. But now, as I sit at the foot of the stairs, it was just a minor hiccup in our past.

I really have to pull myself together before Dad and Maisy get home. I hobble to the bathroom to check out my injuries. Please don't let my face look terrible. I can work through the pain of an injury at gym, but I can't hide my face from Dad, Sam, Quinn ... *the cameras.*

The left side of my face is already badly swollen; I worry about what it'll look like tomorrow. My ribs ache, but thankfully, they don't feel broken. I swipe some thick foundation on my face and mask it all with a thick layer of pressed powder before and rush into the confessional booth. I feel like there's a time bomb attached to me. I need to get in one more segment before tomorrow when I'm certain my face will look like hell. Besides, if there's any way to prepare for Dad's certain round of questioning, it's in front of a camera.

I get in a few minutes of mindless jabbering when Dad knocks on the door.

"Come in," I yell back. I breathe in deeply and hold it longer than I need to. I wonder if he can see anything yet, especially with the bright lights blazing down on me.

We talk for a bit. I'm feeling good about my acting skills. We decide to deal with my car in the morning so that neither of us has to go out in the rain. I'll take his car to gym in the morning. Dad isn't one for fixing things himself, but he'll bring it in, and promises it'll be running by Monday. It's not until I get up from the overstuffed chair and hobble to turn off the lights that dad notices something is off.

"What happened to you, Syd? Did you take a tumble at gym?" he asks.

"Close. I tripped down the stairs after I got out of the shower," I tell him.

He tilts my face each way to inspect it.

"You hurting?"

"My ribs hurt a little," I say. *A lot.*

"Well, you really did a number this time, kid. Do you need me to call the doctor?"

His concern hurts. He doesn't have the energy for this.

"Nah, I'm fine. I am going to turn in early, though," I say. I slowly start up the stairs, holding my ribs in an attempt to minimise the pain.

"You sure you don't need to see a doctor?" he asks. Apprehension fills his voice. I know that I can't tell him how bad it really hurts. I can't tell him that as bad as the pain is, it doesn't touch how bad my heart is aching because Trevor walked out on me. I can't tell him the truth. *Ever.*

"No, no, no. I'll be fine tomorrow. Thanks, Dad, goodnight," I say weakly as I close my door behind me.

I curl up on my bed and the tears start again. Trevor and I were here, together, just a couple of hours ago. Trevor, the person that I *love*. Trust. The person I'd given myself to so wholeheartedly. The person that hurt me, and then walked out on me.

I'm teetering on the ledge of awake and sleep when I hear my phone vibrate on the night stand. I blink several times to clear the grogginess and heavy tears that cloud and burn my eyes.

I'm sorry. I love you and hope you're okay.

I take a deep breath and then reply:

It was my fault. I love you.

My ribs ache. My face is throbbing. I just want things to be okay again. I want all of this hurt to stop. And if that means my taking the blame, well, that's acceptable to me. I let my tears dry and hope for sleep to come soon.

By the time I get home from gym the next day, my car is back in the driveway – just a dead battery according to Dad. The whole situation last night probably could have been avoided if I would have thought of that. I'm certain Grant would have had jumper cables. That fact irritates me. He should have offered to try that, I tell myself. That's it. I'm blaming him now.

Quinn and Tessa both call Sunday to see if I wanted to go shopping, but I'm too sore. I still refuse to see a doctor, even though Ibuprofen isn't touching the pain. I tell them that I don't feel well and am going to be staying in. I really haven't been spending a whole lot

110

of time with my friends lately. I miss them. And more than that, I haven't been giving the producers the social footage they've demanded. Instead, I catch up on taping segments (with lots of makeup on to hide the marks on my face), and catch up on some laundry.

Confessional

"I haven't been working on bars a whole lot this week."

Last time, I wasn't able to do anything other than bar work since I could conceal my injuries with my grips. This time, I can't work on bars because my slamming my ribs into them when I cast makes me feel like I'm splitting my body in half.

"I'm so nervous about Nationals that school has been a great distraction lately."

Trevor has been apologetic and boyfriend-of-the-year material since I accepted responsibility for our argument. It'd been my fault. I shouldn't have accepted the ride from Grant, after all.

Eighteen

Grant's already sitting at our table when I walk into Oceanography on Monday morning. He turns to look at me before I even make it to my seat. His eyes light up momentarily, until I turn my face as I set my things down. I assume by the widening of his eyes, that I haven't done as good of a job covering up the bruised left side of my face, as I thought I had. My lips form a tense smile. I want to play off the injury, but I also don't want to have to talk to him.

I sit down and start organizing my books.

"Sydney," he says tightly.

"Grant," I joke back, trying to mimic his serious tone.

Still, I refuse to look up. I can't. I don't want to look into those eyes.

"Syd, look at me," he says. The way my name sounds coming from his lips is more than I can handle right now.

I give nothing in response. I am frozen.

He lets out an audible sigh and reaches out with a single finger and tilts my chin up so that he can see my face. I don't flinch away, but I still avoid his eyes.

"What the hell happened to you?" Grant demands. His voice is thoughtful but firm.

"I tripped and fell down the stairs at my house," I say with a light laugh.

He's quiet. *Good.* Let's leave it at that.

"I don't believe you," he finally says.

"I tripped, drop it," I say through my teeth.

"Jesus Christ, just wait until I—" His voice is protective and full of anger.

My eyes dart up at his threat. If he confronted Trevor, it would everything. Forever.

"I fell down the stairs. That's it," I say firmly. Tears form in my eyes. My nose and chin burn as I fight them off. *I can't cry.* I'm determined to make Grant believe me.

Grant stares back at me. I can tell by the look in his eyes that he still doesn't buy it.

"Please," I say quietly. "Please. Let it go. For me." My voice has become a tortured beg. *When did I become this person?*

He finally breaks our stare and looks down at his hands. He nods his head once, then turns towards the front of the classroom.

Not another word is spoken between Grant and me.

Confessional

"I've been working on my Arabian Double Front constantly the last few days."

Now that my ribs hardly hurt anymore, I've got a lot of catching up to do.

No one other than Grant even doubted my story about falling down the stairs. Most likely because no one else is quite as perceptive – or nosy – as Grant. Quinn and Tess laughed with me when I recounted the story of how I fell; how someone who is making a career out of having great balance can be such a klutz. Trevor cringed every time someone asked me what happened. It hurt to see him so full of guilt.

"I know I said I'd try to make it happen, and I've succeeded. Here with me tonight is my boyfriend, Trevor."

He's here because he feels guilty, I know that. And I hate that that's the reason, but the producers have really been hounding me for social footage. This was the best I could do. I don't have time to be social right now, surely they understand that.

Trevor smiles uncomfortably and shifts his weight in the chair.

"Nationals are just a week away. I've been prepping so hard for so long. I can't wait to just get there and get the job done."

I'm looking forward to getting out of town for a while. To put all of the drama behind me. Maybe when I come back, it'll be like a real, legitimate fresh start.

"You'll do great, baby." Trevor reaches over and brushes my bangs off of my face and kisses my forehead. *It's showy, and completely not like him, but I'll take it.*

Nineteen

It's been two weeks since Grant and I have spoken.

I nervously wait in front of the school with the rest of our Oceanography class to board the bus for our field trip to the Aquarium. Honestly, I'd debated whether to skip school or not so I could miss the trip. But I haven't had the best test scores lately because I've been so focused on gym and Trevor, so I can't miss the points this trip counts for. I can't believe that this is my life right now. Contemplating missing class. Grades dropping.

I still don't really know anyone in my class, so I take a seat alone, near the front of the bus. Just before the doors close, Grant's tall, tan frame occupies the narrow aisle.

I sigh. I hope he doesn't notice, because it's rude, but I know he'll sit with me.

But he doesn't. And I don't know if I feel relief or disappointment. Everything about my relationship with Grant is confusing. A contradiction. I want him to leave me alone, but when he does I can't help but wish he was next to me instead.

He sits in the only open bench seat, which is right in front of me. His posture is perfectly straight, much more formal than I've seen before. His keeps his back to me the entire ride and I stare at his neck, remembering the clean smell of his skin as he carried me down the stairs. I shake my head, trying to clear my thoughts. I'm glad when he pulls out his iPod and flips open a book, signalling he definitely won't be turning around to acknowledge me.

Despite its relative closeness, the ride to the aquarium takes longer than you'd think because of the heavy traffic. I skim through a few magazines, trying to drown my thoughts with senseless celebrity gossip. Once we get there, I keep my head down as Grant and I both repack our things and avoid the heck out of each other's eyes. I let him make his way out of the bus first, before I even stand and start for the stairs. I turn the corner to take the first step out of the bus, and Grant is there. His hand is extended for me. I narrow my eyes at him.

"Let me help you down," he says. "You know, wouldn't want you to 'fall' again." He makes air quotes around the word fall and I want to scream at him. I glare instead. Why won't he just let this go?

"I really did just fall," I say.

"Whatever you say, Sydney." He shakes his head before walking ahead of me. I have to run to keep up with his long strides.

"What's your problem?" I demand. I feel stupid for chasing him down, but this interfering has got to stop.

"*My* problem?" he asks sharply. He stops walking and stares down at me. I can tell he's waiting for me to argue. Why can't I just walk away? Why do I feel this incredible pull for things to be okay with him? With everyone? The rest of the class has gone inside, and it's just Grant and me out in the large entry way.

"My *problem*," Grant starts, "is that I fucking care about you. And he hurts you. Admit it."

"That's not true. I fell. It was an accident. Can we please just drop this?" I feel the warmth on my cheeks, the trembling in my voice. I wish I was better at hiding my emotions.

"Sydney," he says softly. "Look, please just know that I'm here. If you need anything you just have to ask …" He stumbles over his words and it's so unlike him.

"Okay," I mumble. It's a lie. I'll never be able to do that.

He seems to accept it, though, and we turn towards the entrance.

The rest of the class is already well into the tour. We decide against catching up with them, and instead, take our own tour.

To say that the Atlanta Aquarium is massive is a total under-statement. It's literally the largest aquarium in the world. And I'm here. With Grant.

Now that he's said what's been weighing on his mind, things feel a bit less weird between us, and, actually, it's really nice to be around him again. I know it's wrong to feel so happy to be able to spend this time with him because my being with him is the source of all of the problems that I have with Trevor. But, right now, I don't care.

We walk through the large, acrylic tunnel. It's dark and peaceful and I can't help but enjoy it.

"So, you never finished telling me, what happened with you and your ex?" I try to sound casual rather than nosy.

"Jealous are we?" he says with a smile. I visibly cringe. "I'm kidding, Syd. There's no big story, sometimes, things just don't work out the way that you hope they will."

His words are composed, but I can't help but sense a twinge of regret behind them.

"I guess you're right," I say, and I can't help but think about my relationship with Trevor.

"All right, now it's your turn," Grant says.

"My turn for what?"

"To answer a difficult question."

"Shoot," I say.

"How do your parents feel about Trevor?" he asks. That's *not* the

119

question I was expecting. I decide to keep my answer honest. Simple.

"My dad actually likes him a lot," I say. I look down at a lock of my hair as I twirl it around my finger.

"Hmmm ..." he says. "What about your mom?"

"My mom? Um, she passed away a couple of years ago." The familiar sting in my throat is there when I say the words.

"Shit, Syd, I'm sorry."

Grant takes my hand away from the piece of hair that I've been obsessively twirling and holds it in his.

"It's okay." I shrug. I hate this part. When people feel bad for asking a simple question. Like they should have somehow known. But Grant isn't like most people. He doesn't ask a bunch of questions, and in turn, I find myself offering up information more than usual.

"It was a freak thing. A hit and run. She was out jogging, like she did every single morning before work. Some idiot hit her." I wipe my eyes to make sure they're still dry. "He just left her there."

Like Trevor left me. Injured. Alone.

Grant listens intently as I play it all out for him. The cops showing up at the door and me being the one to answer. How they held up her license, and asked if I knew her. How I said no and slammed the door in their faces. Grant squeezes my hand lightly every time he hears my voice crack. I tell him how my mom is the reason I do gymnastics. How badly she wanted that for me before she died.

"Sometimes, when I'm competing, I feel like she's with me," I say before I can stop the words from tumbling out of my mouth. I feel the rush of embarrassment and regret immediately.

Grant notices the change in my demeanor and shakes his head slowly.

"I bet she's with you all the time, Sydney," he says.

"You think?"

"Absolutely."

"I'm afraid I'm disappointing her," I say.

He laughs, like he can't believe I just said that.

"Why would she be disappointed?"

"I don't know, like I'm not doing things well enough. I barely spend time with my sister. My grades are slipping..." I let my voice trail off when I see him shaking his head again.

"You can't be everything to everyone. I'm sure the only thing you could possibly do to let your mom down is to spend your life unhappy." I know there are several ways I can interpret his statement. That I spend too much time trying to please everyone; trying to live up to everyone else's expectations of me – in gym, in school, at home. Or that I have a sometimes unstable relationship with my boyfriend that isn't healthy ... I'm sure he meant the latter.

"I don't want to talk about this anymore," I say, jumping up off of the bench. I smile widely and motion for him to get up, too. "Let's go check out some more fish!"

He smiles back for a second, but then his forehead creases and his lips curve downward.

"What is it?" I ask.

He points behind me. "Cameras."

"Crap," I say. "Dad or Sam must've told them we'd be here."

"I'm sorry," he says, like it's his fault my life is a total circus.

"Don't be, it's not your fault."

"Do you want me to go somewhere else? Out of their shots, I mean."

Yes.

"No." How can I say yes after I just bared my soul to him. "I want to stop in the gift shop. I bet they can't follow us in there." Grant

121

nods and follows me into the tight space. I stop to inspect the display of snow globes. I'm right; the cameras can't film inside the gift shop, it's too packed in here for them to even attempt a clear shot. Not that I'm that interesting. Geez.

"You collect these?" he asks, picking up a snow globe full of plastic sea horses and star fish.

I shake my head. "No, my sister does. This week anyway."

I find one that has sharks and mermaids. The combo is ridiculous and makes me laugh, so that's the one I decide on. Grant stays close to my side as I go to the register to pay. There's a large glass jewellery case next to the register. My eyes grow wide.

"What? What's the matter?" Grant asks. The concern is ever present in his voice.

"Nothing, it's just …" I point into the locked case. A strand of fresh water pearls is on display on the top shelf. They're almost identical to the ones I'd ruined.

"My mom had some just like that," I say.

"The ones you wore to prom?" he asks. I pull my brows together, wondering how he remembers that.

"I notice everything about you, Sydney," he adds with a shy shrug of his shoulders, answering the unspoken question in my eyes.

"Yeah, those are the ones. But they broke." I frown.

"Next customer, please." The elderly woman behind the counter calls to me. I glance up at Grant's sympathetic eyes and walk to the other side of the counter to make my purchase.

We walk silently toward the exit. I know the cameras are likely behind us. That I should leave Grant's side. But I just don't have it in me to fake it right now. I'm here, with him, because I want to be.

"We need to find the class before we end up stranded in Atlanta," Grant says, resting his hand on the small of my back. He still looks concerned though, ever since I brought up the necklace. He knows there's more to that story than I alluded to. We're walking closer now than we had on the way in to the aquarium. This time, I don't have to imagine the warm, clean smell of his skin; I can breathe it in.

"So, you never did tell me, what happened with you and Shayna after prom," I say. I bump his arm with mine and try to sound blasé, but fail miserably.

Grant lets out a small laugh.

"Actually, if you want to get technical about it, *you* never let me finish telling you," he qualifies.

"Right."

"Nothing happened. If you know me at all, you've got to know that."

"But I saw you two go into the guest room together and then leave together the next morning."

He pinches the skin in between his eyes.

"But nothing happened. She was wasted. I couldn't very well take her home like that, but I sure as shit wasn't going to leave her there, drunk, in a house full of guys, either. So I stayed the night in the room with her after she passed out, but I slept on the floor. I drove her home the next morning. That's it."

"Oh." Is all I can lamely muster. He grins back at me, seeing the surprise on my face.

"Why in the world would you honestly think …" he starts. "Never mind." He throws his head back in a booming laugh that catches me off guard. I can't help but crack a smile and then join in.

We board the bus together, taking the same seats we had on the way to the aquarium – though this time, he doesn't keep his back turned to me. I'm thankful that the bus is filled to capacity with students and teachers so the cameracrew can't board with us. Pulling away from them, and the aquarium, the relief is palpable.

123

"So, what's on your agenda for the summer?" I ask Grant.

"I'm going back to New York," he answers. I feel my face fall at the mention of him leaving town. "Just for a month or so. My mom still has work there and I want to catch up with friends. What about you?"

"I'll be around. I may actually take a little break from gymnastics. Maybe even relax for a change."

"I'd love to see that!" He laughs loudly.

"Hey, I can relax!" I swat his strong arm playfully, but quickly recoil.

"I'm sure you can. Maybe I'll be around to hang out sometime."

I cringe involuntarily.

"Or not," he says, seeing the look on my face. He sounds a little hurt.

"It's not that. It's just—"

"Trevor," he interrupts, flatly.

I nod meekly. The end of the school year is quickly approaching. I only have a few weeks left with Trevor before he graduates. He's been accepted into his first choice school, The University of Georgia. He'll even be playing lacrosse for them. Trevor and I haven't talked much about what will happen with us when he leaves, mostly because we're both so busy, but also, because Athens is less than two hours away, so neither of us has been overly concerned about our relationship changing too drastically. He'll be home on weekends. And holidays. He'll make time to see me, right?

"Sydney," Grant says in a much quieter, more serious tone than our conversation had been in up to this point. The way he breathes my name, with the tiniest bit of pain behind it makes my heart jump. "I meant what I said earlier. I'm here if you need anything."

"I know," I say. Still, I stare down at my lap, unable to look up and meet his gaze. Finally, I peek out from under the protective cover of my hair. "How do you know when enough is enough?" My question is overly broad, but I know he'll understand.

He's quiet for a while. Carefully crafting his response, as usual.

"Well, I think everyone has their own limit, their own breaking point. Until someone reaches that limit on their own, no one can tell them what is right or wrong, or, what you asked, when enough is enough. They just have to figure it out for themselves."

He shrugs and I mull it over for a minute. I'm not exactly sure what I'm asking Grant, or even why. He senses that his answer isn't enough for me.

"You know, when I was a kid, my older brother and I used to wrestle a lot. We only had one rule when we did, and that was that we would stop and let the other go if they yelled 'mercy'. He and I would both hold off saying it as long as we could. Even if the other had gotten out of hand and we were really hurting, we would wait until we absolutely couldn't stand it anymore before we'd say mercy." He's smiling at the memory.

"But if you're asking what I think you are, I don't think relationships should be like our wrestling matches. Relationships are supposed to make you happy, and bring something good to your life. When that stops, for me at least, then it's time to think about moving on. It's just my opinion, of course, but I think you should get out while you still have some peace of mind. Why stick around until you're yelling mercy, you know?" He looks at me.

"But what if you don't have a breaking point?" I ask.

"Everyone has a breaking point, Syd. Some people are just better at putting up with other peoples' crap than most," he says with a slight laugh, lightening the mood again.

The rest of the ride back to school is filled with less serious topics. We pull into the school parking lot just as the final bell is ringing for the day. Grant turns to me again. His messy hair is falling in his face a little more than usual.

"I don't want to complicate your life, Sydney. But I do want to be your friend. I can keep my distance, if that'll make things easier for you, but I really don't want to go back to not even talking."

"I don't want that either," I admit. I'm not sure what the solution is for Grant and me, but I enjoyed our day together too much to go back to not speaking to him for Trevor's sake.

"Friends?" I ask.

"Absolutely," he says, with his absurdly handsome smile. But just as quickly as it crosses his face, it falls again.

"What?" I ask. I'm totally lost as to why his demeanour has changed so quickly.

"Syd, I have to tell you something."

"And I take it it's bad?" I ask. Of course it is. Look at his expression.

"The documentary. I know more than I let on. I mean, I knew about your mom. I'm so sorry I didn't say anything sooner."

My mind is spinning. My mom? How did he know? Why did he pretend not to? Things make even less sense than usual.

"What? How could you know? Who told you?"

The tendons in his neck flex as he swallows deeply.

I'm shaking. What the hell is going on?

"My mom is the producer of the show. I should've told you sooner, I know. I just didn't want to weird you out or anything."

"I don't understand why you're telling me this now then? Because you feel guilty now that I told you all of my secrets?"

He exhales sharply.

"I don't know. Maybe."

He reaches to touch me, but I flinch away. He's left sitting there, staring at me, looking wounded as everyone else filters off of the bus.

126

"It's more than that. I know why they picked you. You said you had no clue why they'd want you for the show, but I know. They chose you because they didn't think you could handle it. That the girl with the dead mom would crack under the pressure of it all. That you'd give them sweeps-worthy television."

I feel like I'm having a panic attack. Like I can't take in enough breath. Like I'm drowning.

"And all this time you knew?" I ask.

He nods.

"And what? You were in cahoots with them? Did you set out to cause trouble between me and Trevor to make good television? Is that why you kissed me? Is that why you've tried to turn my entire life upside down ever since we met? Was it all just to help their cause?"

Everything is spinning. Blackness claws at my peripheral vision. *Breathe, Syd. Breathe.*

"Of course not! That's why I'm telling you now. I just want to be honest with you."

Silence. What more can we say. He's kept this from me for months.

"Back out of the show, Syd," Grant finally says.

"Are you crazy? I can't do that. I signed a contract. And they're paying me a lot of money."

"I'll get you the money, Sydney. I'll ask my mom for it. I'll figure something out. Just back out. It's going to be a smear fest."

I don't know how to even begin to digest all of this. I just need him to go away. I need to be alone and try to figure out how I could have been so stupid to not figure all of this out before. Why did I think the producers would legitimately be interested in me? I just need Grant to leave.

"Thanks for the warning," I say coldly.

Grant walks off the bus and towards his car without looking back.

Confessional

I need to do more of these, even if I know it's already set up to make me look like a freak. Like a failure.

I'm not going to give in that easy.

"I can't believe it's finally here, but I'll be flying to Nashville later this week for Nationals! All of these months of working and it's all for this weekend. I'm really looking forward to getting out there and completing my routines and making my coach proud." If I screw up, Sam is going to lose it. We've been training non-stop, there's no excuse that'll be good enough for me to walk away as anything but the winner. "School has been going well." Grant and I make little more than small talk in class. It should feel better after his confession, knowing that I'm not the only one that's been keeping a secret. But I can't help but feel betrayed. It's easier to pretend that entire conversation never happened. That Grant never confessed that he's been keeping something so big from me. After all, who the heck am I to judge about keeping secrets? I'll deal with it after Nationals. "But I'm looking forward to wrapping up this school year so that I'll have a little break from both training and classes." I'm exhausted.

Twenty

The week flies by at a record pace.

Trevor and I are back to getting along as normally as we ever had. We've had a good, peaceful week, and I think I've almost convinced Dad to let me go to the lake house with Trevor and his family.

I can't quite believe it, but Nationals are this weekend, so I take Thursday and Friday off of school and spend the entire day in gym. I'm completely exhausted from all the extra training and yet totally exhilarated. After all the weeks of hard work, I actually feel ready to go and take on the world.

Sam and I fly to Nashville late Friday night, with Dad and Maisy due to arrive on Sunday in time for the afternoon competition. I find myself secretly wishing they weren't coming at all. I know that makes me a terrible human being, but the added pressure of people in the audience makes everything even more nerve-wracking. I really don't want to let anyone down.

Somehow, I manage to keep my nerves in check and do well in preliminaries on Saturday. I'm even ranked third going into finals on Sunday. After an early morning workout, I walk back to the hotel to sneak in a cat nap. I dig my phone out of my gym bag and check my messages. There's one from Trevor asking how things are going. I smile and send him a quick reply that everything is great and I'll call him later. I set the alarm on my phone and curl up under the flimsy blanket. The room is pitch-black, thanks to the thick, canvas curtains, and I'd turned the air conditioning to its near arctic temperature. Those are all the things that should make it easy to drift off; still I doubt the nerves will allow it.

I'm lying on the cream-coloured sofa in Grant's room, covered in that same comfortable quilt I'd been wrapped up in the night I was sick. Except this time, I'm not alone. Grant's there, lying next to me, with that trademarked messy hair falling in his face. I look at him for a long time, trying to remember why I'm there. My heart is racing at the feeling of his strong arm, pulling me in close at my waist. The warmth and security of it all is intoxicating. His free hand brushes across my face.

"I have to go," I say. Knowing that whatever the reason for my being in his house, *in his room* more precisely, it isn't a good enough one. I'm not even supposed to be talking to him, let along lying in his arms. Trevor will be furious. I have to leave.

Still, looking into Grant's safe eyes, I feel … conflicted.

"Stay," he whispers. He tenderly strokes my face and I can feel the goose bumps rise on my arms.

"I can't. I'm not supposed to be here," I say, pulling away from him.

He gently tugs me back down.

"I don't want you to leave, Syd." He pushes his hair back out of his face, revealing the hurt in his eyes.

"I don't want to leave," I admit. But still, I'm up, and my hand is lingering on the doorknob.

"Then stay."

"But it's so wrong for me to be here."

He's next to me now. It makes it harder to protest with him so close.

"Not if it's what makes you happy," he says. "Stay. Let me take care of you."

I crumble at the adoring look in his eyes. He can tell I've surrendered, because he scoops me up like a small child and carries me back to the couch. My pulse quickens. I can stay. He'll take care of me. I literally feel like I'm shaking with delight.

Not shaking.

Vibrating.

It takes me a moment to realise I've fallen asleep with my phone still clutched in my hand. I don't even check the caller id.

"Hello?" my voices scratches out.

"Sydney? Are you okay?" A voice of concern, just not the one I'd been dreaming about.

"Trevor? Yeah, I'm fine. I just dozed off. Sorry." I pull myself upright and sip a bottle of water, trying to cure my grogginess.

"Okay. I just wanted to wish you luck, and tell you I love you."

Shame washes over me.

"Thank you. I love you too. How are you?" I ask. I'm not ready to hang up now.

"Good, just waiting for you to come home. I don't like when you're away from me."

"I miss you." I mean it.

"Miss you too, Syd. Hey, are you coming to the lake with us next weekend? I never got a straight answer from you."

I smile. He's going to be thrilled.

"Yeah, I am, actually. I can't believe I've been so busy I forgot to tell you. I can't stay Saturday night, though, it's Maisy's birthday. But Friday night, I'm all yours."

"That's perfect," he says. "I can't wait to see you. Love you, baby."

We hang up and I toss the phone onto the nightstand and

stretch. At the same moment, Sam pounds on the door to wake me up.

The arena is too cold. I know I'll be fine once I start moving around, but right now the frigid air isn't helping my nerves. The feeling of elitism is practically visible in the air. Every gymnast here feels that they're truly better than the one next to them, not just the gym. It's always harder on me to come in to finals near the top. There are more people watching you. It's easier, for me at least, to come in from behind, where no one is expecting anything from you.

Of course, the constant cameras trailing me don't make blending into the background any easier. And, just like at school, I'm either scowled at, or people that generally don't know I exist are now my best friends in order to cement their chance of being on TV.

Vault is my first event, which in itself does a number on my stress level. I stand off to the side of the runway, waiting for my turn. I run through each movement of my vault in my head while my competitors go. The gymnast in front of me sits down her landing and I can't help but cringe. It should be a relief to me that she'd done so poorly, but I feel bad. I know, just like everyone else in this arena, all of the hours that have gone into her making it here. To fall is such a huge blow to your confidence.

I smile sympathetically as she passes me on my way up the short flight of steps to the vaulting runway. She glares back with stabby eyes. I'm taken aback by her wicked scowl and almost lose my footing on the padded steps. I grab at the railing, righting myself before I fall. I giggle to myself, thinking of the first day that I met Grant. I really need to stop thinking about him.

I float gracefully to the end of the runway and stare at the vault. Running full speed at a stationary object has never been my favourite thing. *You can do this, Sydney. You can do this.* The judges raise the green flag and I throw my arms up to salute them.

I bound towards the vaulting table. Hurdle. Round-off. My feet pound into the springboard. I throw my arms back. Back hand spring onto the vault. My fingertips press into the vault, as I push myself high into the air. Twisting. Once. Twice. Until I land, digging my feet firmly into the mat. I raise my arms above my head to salute the judges. I scan the sideline for Sam. When I finally lay eyes on him, he's beaming. One event down, three to go.

I do reasonably well on balance beam and uneven bars. I'm glad we added the extra difficulty into my bar routine. Maybe I even hated the dismount a little less today. Maybe.

I'm in second place as we head into the last rotation, floor exercise. As long as I don't totally screw up, I really have a shot at winning this thing.

The sound of my music drifts through the huge arena. My nerves are gone as I dance and tumble across the large mat. One final tumbling pass and I'll be finished. I put every ounce of power into my last tumbling run.

Too much power.

I land perfectly, feet slamming into the mat.

Out of bounds.

My heart sinks as I watch the judge raise the red flag alerting everyone to my mistake. I finish the routine with a plastic smile and walk off the podium.

Sam is upset. I don't blame him. I didn't spend all of this time and put in all of this work to lose with such a stupid mistake.

When my score is revealed, Sam grimaces. I immediately think of Dad and Maisy up in the stands. I don't bother looking for them. I don't want to see the disappointment firsthand.

Everyone else holds their own on floor. And when the competition is over, I still manage to medal. Just not the colour I wanted. I stand on the lowest podium, the third place, bronze medal spot. Sam's temper has cooled down. He says maybe next year will be my year. But my disappointment in myself doesn't fade as quickly.

We all fly home together. Even the camera crew assigned to me is on our flight. I close my eyes and pretend to sleep the entire way. No matter what I've done lately, it seems like everything I've tried so hard to keep together is falling apart.

I want to be a good sister to Maisy and make up for my mom's absence, but I'm failing miserably at that, she won't even speak to me most days; I want to be a great gymnast, but I have trouble keeping my footing just walking up a couple of steps; I want to be an incredible girlfriend to Trevor, but I can't make him happy and earlier today I was dreaming about some other guy that Trevor hates beyond words. I'm overwhelmed by the heaviness of it all.

Maybe I need to come clean to Trevor. Tell him that Grant and I are sort-of friends now. Let the chips fall where they may. I ponder that thought while I feign sleep, but realise quickly that the chips will likely fall with Trevor breaking up with me. And despite our fights, I don't want that to happen. I wish I could talk to Quinn about things, but she'd be so one-sided. She never liked Trevor to begin with, so if she knew what was going on behind the scenes, she'd never let it go. Tess would be a good confidant, but I barely see her anymore now that she and Oliver are dating. And could I really trust her not to tell Quinn?

We get home late. Dad says I don't have to go to school in the morning, so naturally, Maisy is upset that the same offer doesn't apply to her. I debate whether to go or not as I fall asleep. I know one thing for certain – I won't be going to gym in the morning.

Twenty-one

I don't make it out of bed early the next morning. In fact, I don't make it out of bed before lunch. I wake up with the sun streaming heavily through the thin curtains – a dead giveaway I've overslept. I tilt the alarm clock so that I can read it. 2:25 P.M. I groan and grab my phone off of the night stand.

Seven missed calls.

One is from Quinn and Tess both chiming in on speaker phone, full of laughter and happiness. Asking if I'm okay and congratulating me on my medal.

There are six messages from Trevor.

I glance at the clock again. School will be out soon and I don't want to be sitting at the house if any unsolicited visitors decide to stop by. I throw on some clothes, brush my teeth and bolt out the door.

I purposely leave my phone on my bed. Relief settles in deeper as I watch my house shrink in the rearview mirror. I have no clue where I'm going. I just roll down the window and let the thick air fill the car. It blows my hair into a knotted mess and clears my head. It feels amazing. Most of all, it feels *real*.

No Trevor. No Sam. No cameras.

I drive around aimlessly for hours, until the sun starts to set. I decide I'd better get home before my dad calls out a search party. He always gets anxious when I'm gone and don't leave a note. I hadn't intended on being gone so long. But I did come to a few conclusions as I drove around.

Decision one is that Grant had been a good friend to me. And for whatever reason, I can't walk away from our friendship. Even if he didn't initially tell me who his mom was, I feel a strong connection to him. One that I'm not willing to give up. Trevor will have to find a way to accept it. I hope.

Second, I love Trevor. I want things to be good with us again. I want to make him happy. And I'm going to be honest with him. I'm going to tell him about my friendship with Grant. I have to make him see that we're just friends. That I'm one-hundred-percent committed to him. And no one will sway that.

Third, I can't put my finger on it, but the last few months, I really feel like I've lost a part of myself. Maybe Trevor and Grant were both right (for different reasons); maybe the documentary was a bad idea. It will be over soon. And when it is, I'd like to go back to being me. Except this time, a version of me that doesn't always have to put gym – and everyone else first. I want to have friends again. That's not too much to ask, right? I miss Tessa and Quinn. I want to hang with my friends, and sleep in on weekends, and just be me. And though I haven't felt normal in a long, long time, I want that more than anything. And somehow when this is all over with, I'll get *me* back.

I wake up early the next morning. Sam did say I could take the rest of the week off from gym, but I'm feeling lazy and sore, so I decide to go in for a short workout anyway. Plus, the extra time I'll have to get my thoughts in order will be a good thing.

When I got home the night before, I didn't check my phone for missed calls. I wasn't ready to deal with anyone. I even purposely get to school just before the bell rings. It's become a habit: trying to avoid having to see anyone on my way to class lately. Unfortunately, my plan doesn't work and Trevor is waiting for me right outside of my first class.

I slow my walk when I see him standing by the door. He's leaning against the wall, his hands shoved into his jeans pockets. He has sunglasses on so I can't see his eyes, but still, he looks a little sad. I immediately regret ignoring him the last couple of days. Even if I am thankful for the time I've had to get my thoughts in order, seeing him so down makes me second-guess all of my decisions. I'm slightly relieved to see that his face brightens when he spots me.

"Hey!" he says, walking up to meet me.

"Hi," I say, nervously. I pick at a piece of my jumper that's unraveled a bit, trying my best to avoid eye contact.

"Where've you been? I've been so damn worried about you. I called and called. I even stopped by your house last night but your dad said he didn't know where you were. What's going on?" He speaks so quickly that all of his words run together and his brief smile fades.

"I'm sorry about that. I was just so disappointed about not doing so well at Nationals. I didn't want to face anyone right away." It's true.

He ponders this for a minute.

"I saw that you screwed up. Sorry you lost," he says. His choice of words is a stinging barb to my heart.

"Listen, I'm gonna be late for class," I motion towards the classroom door.

He doesn't respond. Instead, he pulls me in close and crushes his mouth onto mine. It's a way heavier kiss than is appropriate for school. I try to pull away, but he pulls back tighter, pressing his mouth harder on to mine. The warmth of his lips is familiar, and yet somehow, it's forced. Raw. Urgent. He finally releases me and flashes a broad, satisfied smile. I'm momentarily confused by his expression, until I see Grant pause at the door before walking into class. The kiss and the smile all make perfect sense. They weren't for my benefit, but for Grant to see.

I glare up at Trevor. He's still smirking.

"Bye," I say firmly and walk away from him.

"Syd!" he calls after me. He grabs my hand and spins me back towards him. I don't want to fight. I just want to go to class.

"Don't be upset. I just missed you. I just got carried away." He looks at me with an apologetic smile that, if I didn't know him better, would appear sincere. But I know he isn't sorry.

"Okay. I really have to go," I say. I want to go home and go back to bed. I should have known that coming today would be a mistake.

"I love you," he says, totally oblivious to my mood.

"Love you," I stand on my tip-toes and peck him on the cheek.

Grant is already sitting down, reading as usual. I honestly don't have a clue what to say to him. I feel like an idiot because of Trevor's little production just now. Especially after the last time we really talked. That bus ride home seems like eons ago. I'm relieved when he only glances up and smiles quickly before looking back down at his book. Maybe silence is better for us.

Mrs Drez calls the class to order and begins her lecture. I take better notes today than I think I ever have. I'm nervous and want to concentrate on something other than Trevor or Grant.

The entire period is filled with uncomfortable silence. All of the things we want to say hang above us. I *want* to apologise for the PDA. But logically, what would I be apologising for? Trevor's my boyfriend, I wasn't doing anything wrong. So, why does it feel that way when it comes to Grant? I make my way for the door as soon as the bell rings.

I've just made it to the door when I feel someone clutch my elbow.

"Hey," I say to Grant. I shrug out of his light grip.

"Hi, Syd. I know we left things kind of weird with my mom and—" He runs his hand over the scruff on his cheek.

"Stop. It's okay," I say. I don't want to hold on to anymore anger about anything.

He sighs and looks relieved. "And you're okay?"

"Yeah, I guess."

"I watched your competition on TV. You did amazing! Congratulations." His polite offer of congratulations makes me frown.

"What's with the frown?" he asks.

"Um, I'm not sure you were watching the right thing. I sort of lost, Grant." I say.

"Sydney, Sydney, Sydney," he laughs and shakes his finger as if he's scolding me. "I would hardly call being the third best gymnast in the entire country losing. Why are you so damn hard on yourself?"

"Yeah, but—" I start. Before I can finish, he presses his warm index finger to my lips to shush me. Immediately my eyes dart nervously around the campus to see if Trevor ... or *anyone* is watching. I lightly brush his finger away from my face and don't finish my sentence.

"So, we're okay now, right?" he asks.

"Yep." I smile.

"Hey, what are you doing tonight?" he asks as if he hasn't even noticed my uneasiness. I'm glad we're off the subject of gymnastics, but the new question has totally caught me off-guard.

"I have gym tonight." I stare at my top while I zip it up and down repeatedly, trying to distract myself and keep my nerves from taking over.

"After that?" he presses. "Since we agreed to be friends and all."

Is he challenging me? Seeing if I have the nerve to actually hang out with him. Trying to get me to prove that we're really friends?

"I don't have anything after that. Why, what's up?"

He smiles over the fact that I've accepted his dare.

"Nothing major. I just have a little something for you. Think you can you stop by on your way home from gym?" The confidence has returned to his voice now.

"Something for me?" I ask, willing my heart not to beat out of my chest.

"Just a little congrats gift." He holds the door to our next class open for me.

"You so didn't have to do that," I say. My cheeks are scorching little balls of molten lava.

No one has ever bought me a gift for *losing* a meet.

"I know I didn't *have* to, I wanted to. So, you'll stop by?"

Like I could even refuse a smile like that.

I nod in response as I take my seat.

I pull in the large circular driveway at Grant's house with the same nerves I had the first time I came here. I check my makeup in the mirror on my visor once more, then pin my fringe back neatly in a tiny braid along the front of my face, all the while, questioning why I'm bothering.

I walk slowly up the large steps that lead to the front door. Something glowing catches my eye. On each side of every step there are little green, glowing tubes. What in the world? I bend down and pick one up. Glow sticks. Like the kind that you get at Halloween, or from amusement parks at night. I stand there holding the tube, completely puzzled as to why they are lining the walkway, when the front door swings open.

Grant stands in the massive doorway, and a coy smirk decorates his face.

"Hi there," he greets me.

"What's with the glow sticks?" I ask.

His small smirk stretches into a large, amused grin.

"Well, with your track record on stairs, and it being dark, I figured I'd help you out," he says with a wink.

"These are for my benefit?" My brows pinch together.

"Well, yeah. I figured flares would have been just a little over the top," he says with a laugh. He runs his fingers through his thick hair. He's so ridiculously handsome. Especially when you throw in that deep, genuine laugh.

"Oh, you've got jokes tonight?" I say, now laughing with him. I have to admit, it is clever, even if it's at my expense.

"Well, you are awfully delicate," he says. His tone is gentle and serious now. "Are you hungry? Maybe we should grab something to eat first?"

"Um, sure." I wasn't expecting dinner.

He leads me to the garage and opens the passenger door to his car for me. I sink into the comfortable leather seat. Grant slides sinuously into the driver's seat and backs the car out of the driveway.

"Anywhere in particular you want to go?" He's cheerful and relaxed. It's such a nice change.

I shake my head. "No, I'm too indecisive. You pick."

He nods.

"Are you glad school's almost over?" I ask.

"Eh, it depends," he answers cryptically. He turns the car off of the interstate now and I feel a little pang of anxiety when I realise we're staying close to town. What if we're seen out together?

"Depends on what?"

"Well, are you going to be allowed to see me over the summer? Or do I have to hope that we have a class together next year before I see you again?" he has a smirk on his face, but for once, I don't think it's real.

"That's not fair." I'm suddenly uncomfortable. He narrows his eyes at me.

"Maybe. But it's a legitimate question."

"Trevor isn't a bad guy, Grant. He's just stressed. He's got a lot on his plate with lacrosse and college. He just doesn't like sharing me, I guess. But, for your information, I plan on telling him that you and I are still friends this weekend," I inform him smugly. It doesn't feel nearly as good as I thought it would.

"Maybe you should let me be there when you break the news to him," Grant says. His expression is serious. Maybe even a little pained.

"Yeah, I don't think that's such a good idea." I crack a smile to lighten the mood. He doesn't reciprocate. I nudge his right hand that rests on the centre console with mine, hoping it'll make him smile. He clutches my hand in his for a split second, squeezing it tenderly before letting go. Even though his hand is warm, his touch still immediately gives me goose bumps. We pull into a parking space, and, though I know where we are, it takes me a moment to get my bearings. Because I've never been anywhere alone with Grant.

Marietta Square. But at a far different place than I'd been with Trevor. Grant's taken me to a laid-back pizza place. I laugh to myself at the difference between Trevor and Grant's preferences. Except for one thing. Me.

"Is this okay?" Grant asks.

"This is perfect. I haven't had pizza in … I don't even remember when the last time was." It's not exactly an 'approved' food while training.

Grant's hand rests protectively on the small of my back as we cross the parking lot, and when he opens the door, he pauses to let me pass first.

It's an old-fashioned pizza joint, with checkered table cloths, and the best pizza I've ever tasted. It's comfortable. As is the company.

"Are you ready for the Econ final? It looks like it's going to be killer," he says.

I stretch my short legs out on to the bench that he's sitting on and smile at the casualness of it all.

"I think so. I actually really like that class."

"What do you have planned this weekend?"

"It's my little sister, Maisy's birthday. She's having a slumber party, so guess who is in charge of that?" I grin. I conveniently leave out the part about staying the night with Trevor Friday and I feel like a liar for it. "How about you?"

"Not much. My mom will be back in town."

His mom. My producer.

"Don't let it be weird, Syd," he says, seeing the look on my face. "She's got a party planned."

I nod back at him. "What's the occasion?"

He glances away, which strikes me as odd. He always looks me in the eye. Always.

"Nothing really."

I'm certain there's more to it, but I don't want to spoil the mood. But with every smile, every wink, every breeze of his fingers on mine, I'm more and more conscious of how much I need to be honest with Trevor. If I tell Trevor about my friendship with Grant, and he still forbids me to spend time with him, I'm not sure if I can do it. The peacefulness and comfort I feel when I'm with Grant is almost addictive.

When we get back to his house, Julie is busy putting up groceries.

"Hi, Julie," I greet her.

"Hey, Sydney. Good to see you around here again. Did you guys go out for a birthday dinner?" She smiles at Grant.

"Birthday?" I take a minute to process what she's said. "Grant, it's your birthday?"

Grant runs his hand through his hair and laughs, but it's stiff and uncomfortable, not like his usual carefree laugh. The awkwardness in the restaurant makes so much more sense now. Wow. He apparently enjoys attention even less than I do.

"Nice, Jules," he says.

Julie shrugs, closes the refrigerator, and walks quickly out of the room.

"Why didn't you tell me it was your birthday?" I ask.

He shrugs. "Because it doesn't really matter."

"Of course it does! I feel like such a jerk. You just bought *me* dinner on *your* birthday!"

"Come on upstairs. I've got something for you, remember?" he says. He grabs my hand and leads me out of the kitchen. His long fingers intertwine with mine in that perfect way that makes me never want to let go. But I have to.

"Oh yes, presents for me, too. That's just perfect."

He stops halfway up the stairs and turns to me. He presses his index finger to my lips.

"Stop it, Sydney. Don't try to find something else in the world to feel bad about. Just come upstairs. Please."

I fold my arms across my chest and push out a pouty lip in defeat.

"Just humour me," he murmurs irresistibly.

"Well, happy birthday, anyway," I say. I uncross my arms and follow him up the large staircase.

Once inside his room, I plop down onto the comfy sofa. He smiles at me approvingly, pleased by my level of comfort in his space.

"Thanks for going out with me tonight," Grant says. He pulls open one of his desk drawers.

"Thanks for spending your birthday with me."

He sits next to me on the sofa. It's wildly inappropriate how good it feels to be this close to him.

"I spent my birthday exactly how I wanted to."

I can feel his warm breath on my face. I look at him. At his perfectly, unruly hair, a total contradiction, just like our entire relationship. At the small, brown, braided necklace he always wears. At the collar of his brown t-shirt under his white button-up. I look everywhere but his eyes. I know that if I meet his gaze, I will surely lose what little self-control I have and end up making a fool out of myself.

Without a word, he lightly places a small box on my lap. It's about the size of a book, wrapped neatly in crisp, navy paper and a dainty silver ribbon. I hope it's a book. Something simple and impersonal. I can handle a book.

"You really shouldn't have done this. I don't deserve it," I say.

"Yes, you do. Besides, I told you, I wanted to. I hope you like it."

I untie the thin ribbon and lay it neatly across my lap. I feel uneasy with him sitting right next to me, watching me. I move in slow motion, carefully opening each side of the paper and gently pealing it back. Inside is a dark blue, velvet box that I recognise immediately. It's the same type of box that Maisy's snow globe was put in after I bought it from the aquarium. My heart slams in my chest when I realise what must be inside. It's definitely not a book. Tears already start to brim in my eyes before I can even get the box open.

"Don't cry, Syd." He nudges my hands. "I can take them back, if you want."

Inside is the elegant strand of freshwater pearls. The strand that's somehow almost identical to Mom's. The one I'd destroyed in my argument with Trevor.

"No. I just, I just don't know what to say. Thank you so much." I dab at the tears in my eyes with the corner of my sleeve before they can fall.

"You're welcome," he says.

"I really can't believe you did this." My voice cracks with emotion. I finally look up and meet his eyes. His expression is warm. His eyes are full of empathy and affection. My self-control is slipping. Teetering. Breaking. I can't help it. I reach up and run my hand through his hair. His eyes close and he lets out a barely audible sigh. I jerk my hand back and close it in my lap. What am I doing? I glance at my watch nervously. I had told Dad that I was going to do some homework with a friend. I didn't anticipate dinner.

"I should go," I say. I start for the bedroom door. I know I'm being rude. I don't really want to leave. I wonder if Grant can sense that. Surely he'll understand. He's never had any trouble deciphering my moods.

"Hey, Syd, I hope I didn't upset you."

This is by far the most thoughtful, generous thing anyone has ever done for me. So, upset? No. Definitely not.

"You didn't, I just have to go." I turn for the door and run down the stairs.

I hope he doesn't follow me. I don't want him to walk me to my car. I don't want to say good-bye to him. I don't even want to look at him again. I know that if any of those things happen, I will kiss him for sure. Because I *want* to kiss him.

I bolt out the front door and don't look back. I'm pretty sure I left him at the top of the staircase questioning my sanity. Once I reach the end of Grant's street, I roll the windows down and let the cool air fill my car.

Dad is at the kitchen table, rubbing his eyes and looking more than stressed when I get home.

I should have called to let him know I'd be later than I'd planned.

"Hey, Dad." I set my gym bag and backpack down on the bar. I try

146

to gauge how much trouble I'm about to be in by the tight look on his face.

"Hi, Syd. Sit down. We need to talk." He points to the wooden chair across from him. My stomach does a flip-flop. I'm never in trouble, but I'm pretty sure that my night with Grant was worth any punishment I'm about to have thrown at me.

"Listen, Dad, I'm really sorry for being late." I leave it at that. I don't have a good excuse, so I don't bother trying to defend myself.

"Late? What time is it?" He glances at the clock above the stove. *Crap, why didn't I just keep my mouth shut?*

"Well, as long as you got your homework done, it's okay. This time."

I let out a sigh of relief. But it's short lived. Because if Dad wasn't upset about me being late, what is going on?

"Syd, I know you've got plans with Trevor and his family this weekend, but I really need your help. I've got to fly to Chicago in the morning to put out some fires. I won't be back until Monday. I really hate to do this to you, darlin', but I need you to stay with Maisy. I don't want her to have to cancel her party."

Me. Solely in charge of my little sister with the super-sized attitude and eight of her friends. Ugh.

"Sure, Dad. No problem." The dutiful daughter saves the day again.

After Dad and I sort out details, I rush upstairs. I'm thankful I don't have a lot of homework, since I didn't even start it. After washing my face and throwing on some pajamas, I flop down on my bed and start to empty my backpack. I guess reading a few chapters in my Econ book isn't a bad idea. On top of my books is the soft blue box. I run my hand across the thick velvet and then crack it open. I trace the elegant line of pearls with my finger. Grant's generosity is unbelievable. I totally didn't deserve this.

I'd rushed out of the house so fast after opening the gift, I hadn't noticed a small note card tucked into a flap on the inside of the box. I pull out the thick cardstock and read the handwritten note.

I laugh out loud when I read his words. Simple. To the point. Just as he always is.

Yes, you do.

-Grant

I slip the note back into its sleeve. How is it that he knows me so well? He gets me like no one else. Something that Quinn had said about Trevor months ago pops back into my head. *"I just don't think he gets you the way that he should."*

Maybe Quinn was more insightful than I'd given her credit for.

Twenty-two

I lay in bed, restless. The nerves twist knots in my stomach before I finally give up on sleeping anymore and get up for the day. I'm so apprehensive about telling Trevor that I can't go to the lake. I know he's going to be upset. And really, I'm concerned about *how* upset he might get.

I could stay home. Dad's already left for the airport. I could tell him I'm not feeling well. I could leave Trevor a message while he's in class. But if I stay home, I won't see Grant. And he'll think I'm upset about his gift. And that's just not acceptable.

There's a note from Dad on the counter for Maisy, explaining that, despite what she thinks, I'm in charge for the weekend. It's written exactly how he would speak to her in person, and that makes me laugh.

I try to take my time getting ready for school after gym. I flat iron my hair and carefully apply the little makeup that I do wear. Still, I manage to arrive at school earlier than usual.

Since I'm early, there's really no point in putting off the inevitable. So I trudge across the quad to find Trevor. Seeing him in the morning used to be the highlight of my day. But now, walking to class with him has turned into something I almost dread. I'm just argued out. I'm tired. I don't want to fight anymore. But with Trevor's temper lately, I don't think I can avoid one today.

He's there. In his usual spot. Surrounded by his large group of friends. Watching him from far away, I'm taken aback by how handsome he is. I remember how it felt in the beginning of our relationship, being seen with him. The way it felt to be *his*. The way I used to love that he never wanted to share me. Because being Trevor's girlfriend was always something that I took pride in. *Was*.

I feel a crushing sadness now when I look at him. He's still gorgeous. His smile is brilliant. He oozes charm. He's still the guy that every girl wants. The guy that, somehow, I managed to snag. Still, despite my best efforts, I can't seem to make him happy. Maybe that's the point. I truly wasn't ever good enough for him.

I now know, looking at Trevor, that things with us are not what they used to be. We can't go back. And maybe I don't even want to anymore. Not aching for Trevor is a foreign feeling to me. I never imagined a time that I wouldn't fight to hang on to what we had.

He finally looks up and sees me watching him. He breaks away from his group of friends to catch up to me.

"Morning, baby." He wraps his familiar arms around my waist and kisses me lightly.

"Morning," I say. I will my voice to sound normal. Whatever normal is for Trevor and me anymore.

"We're taking off right after school, you all packed?" He asks with a level of excitement that makes me cringe.

I stop in the hall and look around. Fortunately, no one is close by. I think carefully about my wording. I try to choose something that won't upset him. I can't come up with anything.

"Listen—" I begin.

"Sydney, please tell me you aren't cancelling. We've had these plans forever. I need to be able to spend some time with you." His voice is pleading. At least he's still smiling; that's a good sign.

"I know, and I want to go. It's just that my dad is out of town. I need to stay with Maisy for the weekend," I say. I rest my hand lightly on his firm chest.

"So, you're staying home to babysit? That's ridiculous. Can't she stay with a friend or something?"

"It's her birthday," I say.

"Dammit, Sydney! I can't believe you're doing this." His smile is gone. His voice has turned cold. I understand that he's upset, but the sulking is aggravating.

"Trevor, be reasonable. I'm not breaking plans on purpose. You know I want to go." I move my hand from his chest to his arm and rub it lightly.

"Do you?" His voice is sharp and he shoves my hand away from him.

"Of course I do. What's that supposed to mean?" Tears are welling up in my eyes, but I fight them. I'm not going to cry at school like an idiot.

"You've been pushing me away for months. And now, this? I just can't help but think—"

He pauses as if he's debating whether or not to finish his thought.

"What? You can't help but think what?" I ask.

"Is there someone else?"

The air leaves me.

"Are you kidding me? I'm not going to do this right now." My voice cracks. *Don't you dare cry.*

"Fine. We'll talk about it later." His voice is low, but still sharp. I assume it's because the bell is about to ring and the hall is much more crowded than it was just a couple of minutes ago.

He leans in to kiss me goodbye, but I turn my head. I don't want to kiss him. He grabs the top of my arm. Hard. The pressure of his fingers wrapped tightly around my slight arm is almost unbearable. I try to twist free, but just as in the past, it isn't working.

He leans in close to me with a fake smile plastered wide on his face. His grip doesn't loosen. I can feel his breath hot on my face. His eyes swim with red, fiery anger.

"Do. Not. Make. A. Fool. Out. Of. Me." He hisses each word through the frightening, plastic smile.

He drops my arm and it falls limply to my side.

I stand there. Stunned. And watch him walk away.

I try to stay composed. But I can feel the heat burning under my cheeks and the salty tears forming in my eyes. My throat tightens up as I fight them back. I quickly glance around to see if anyone saw our argument, but it looks like we've gone unnoticed. I coolly smooth my shirt and hair and walk into class.

I sit down at the empty lab table and stare straight ahead. My mind is racing. It's on a loop, replaying the argument. This one. The others. Too many to keep track of now. I try to block out the image of Trevor in my face, so incensed. Instead, I concentrate on slowing my breathing like I do before a meet. *Clear your head, Syd.*

I just about have it under control when Grant appears and, not surprisingly, it picks right back up. It's not logical that, even in my stress, his presence thrills me the way it does. He smiles warmly as he sets his books down. I give a weak smile back and his fades. His eyes narrow, questioning me silently.

He sits and positions his chair close to mine.

"What's the matter?" he whispers. His head is tilted right next to mine.

"Just tired, I guess." I try to sound nonchalant, but doubt that my mediocre acting skills will be enough to fool him.

I cross my arms on the table top and rest my head in them, wishing I could disappear. My hair falls around my face, blocking me from Grant's gaze. I know it's a wasted effort. I could put a cement wall between us and he'd still see right through me. He reaches over and lightly brushes the hair away from my eyes. The path that his finger has left on my forehead triggers a chill. His gaze is locked on mine, his eyes, full of worry. I know him. I know he isn't going to give up. I have to give him something, but if I really start talking, I'll break down.

I'm teetering. Scared. Alone.

"It's just been a bad day already. I don't really want to talk about it," I say.

"Understood," he nods. Relief fills me as he turns to face forward. He's respectful enough to leave it alone.

Since the school year is wrapping up, there isn't any new material to cover in class. Mrs Drez gives us the period to review for our final. I skim my notes for several minutes, until the painful silence between me and Grant is too much.

"Thank you, again, for the necklace. I really didn't deserve it," I say. My words remind me of the card. A smile tugs at his mouth.

"Yes, you do."

"So, your mom is coming home this weekend?"

"Yeah, she'll be here tomorrow."

"Does she know?" I ask. "I mean, does she know that you and I are friends?"

Grant nods.

"Is she okay with that?"

"Does it matter?" he asks. I wish it were that simple for me to disregard others' opinions. He sighs. "She doesn't care as long as I don't interfere with her show. And if I do, well, I don't care."

"Well, I'm sure it'll be nice to have her home."

"Sure, I guess. What about you? You have your sister's party tomorrow? What about tonight?"

Not going to the lake with Trevor.

"Nothing, just staying in. My dad had to leave town for work, so I'll be home with Maisy."

The rest of the period passes quickly. Rather than rush out of class like I typically do, I gather my things slowly. I hang back, hoping Grant won't leave and we can walk together. Even if that's completely crazy.

"Ready?" he asks.

We walk slowly to class. I fight the urge to look over my shoulder. Even if Trevor is around the corner, this is school. He's not going to cause a huge scene.

"It's too bad you have to stay home all weekend. You could have come over to meet my mom," Grant says.

"Ha!" I laugh. "I'm sure you're mom has had her fill of me on film, she wouldn't be interested in spending time with me socially. Besides, she's been gone for a long time, right? I don't think I should intrude."

Grant stops for a moment. "You could never be an intrusion."

The halls are congested with students hurrying to their next class. We take a more leisurely pace. When the crowd becomes too thick for us to walk side by side, Grant pauses to let me walk in front of him, his hand never leaving its protective spot on my hip.

"So, are you going to tell me what had you so upset this morning?" he asks.

"I don't think so. It's not worth getting into." I glance up to gauge his reaction.

"Fair enough. As long as you're all right." He nudges me lightly with his broad shoulder. The goosebumps that I feel each time he barely touches me are becoming more familiar and expected.

"You know what? I really am."

He doesn't reply. I stop in the hall and look up at him. His smile has faded.

"What's the matter?" I ask.

His only reply is to shake his head. The bell rings.

"We're late," I say.

Grant reaches for me at the same time someone unexpectedly tugs on my arm. I spin around to investigate the source.

Trevor.

"What the hell are you doing?" he yells at me. Trevor yanks me backward with a powerful jolt. With little effort on his part, I'm no longer standing next to Grant.

"Let go of her," Grant says. His words are controlled but firm.

"You, stay the fuck out of it," Trevor shouts back. There's zero restraint in his voice.

"Let me go, Trevor," I plead. I stare at him, trying to see past the anger that encompasses him now. Trying to see the person that I'd fallen in love with. The one person that I'd given myself to. If I could just recognise that person, maybe I could relate to him well enough to get him to stop acting like this. But it's hard to concentrate on anything while his fingers crush into my skin.

"I just want to talk to you," he says. I can't respond.

"I don't think so," Grant says. He's beside me again.

Grant is several inches taller than Trevor and he's glaring down at him with an intensity that I've never seen in him before. If Trevor doesn't let go of me, Grant will make him. His eyes prove it.

Trevor finally relents and drops my arm. I feel it tingle and throb as the blood starts flowing through my veins again.

"Can we please go and talk. You and me?" Trevor asks. His voice is calmer now. Surely a side effect of Grant's presence.

"Yeah, there's no way in *hell* that's going to happen," Grant says. Trevor shoots him another challenging look.

This is not happening. This can't be happening.

"It's okay," I say. This has to stop. "I'll be okay."

I look at Grant. He shakes his head back and forth repeatedly.

"Really," I press.

"Syd, I can't just—" Grant begins.

"She said she's fine," Trevor interrupts. His hand reaches out for mine. I don't want to take it. I don't want to touch him.

He doesn't give me chills. I don't feel protected by his touch, instead, I've come to fear it. But, stubbornly, I want to convince Grant that I'll be all right. I want him to leave. I don't want him to see this part of my life. The messy part. He's already too involved in all of this drama as it is.

"You're late for class," I say to Grant. He continues to stare at me; his face is full of pain and doubt.

I hesitantly take Trevor's outstretched palm, as the final sign that I'm really okay. That I'm where I want to be, and with who I want to be with. This farce hurts me more than any of the other acts I've had to keep up the last few months. This is the hardest to fake. I'm the only one of the three of us that knows for sure that it's not true.

The pain in Grant's face as he concedes and walks away rips at my heart, shreds it. Grant doesn't turn around as he walks away from us. He backs away, like it's against everything in him to leave me standing there. With this person he knows has hurt me. And maybe will again.

I feel myself deflate when Grant is forced to turn a corner and I can no longer see him.

But I can finally drop the act, and Trevor's hand.

"What?" I ask. I force authority to fill my normally meek voice. But my arms, hugging my own chest in a futile attempt to conceal the fact that I'm shaking, contradicts the sound. The halls are vacant. Just me and Trevor. I'm seriously starting to doubt my decision to send Grant away.

"I'm sorry about this morning," Trevor says. His voice is shaky and tense and he looks like he might cry. But really, I've almost come to expect the theatrics from him.

"Okay." Is all that I can offer in response.

"Really, Syd. I was disappointed. I'm sorry that I upset you."

The same boyish face that I longed to forgive a year ago is back. The one who said he loved me and wiped away any doubt I had in us. How did we end up here?

"Forgive me?" He reaches out and tilts my chin up. But I pull back and look at the ground. I can't meet his eyes. I can't say what I need to say while I'm looking at him. I'm a coward.

"Look, Trevor." My voice is barely audible. "I think we may need a little—"

"No," he cuts me off indignantly.

"Trevor—" I start again.

"No, Syd. Don't even say it. The last thing we need is time. Or space. Or whatever generic bullshit line you're about to feed me. Don't do this."

"Let's just take the weekend . . ."

"Syd. I fucking love you. Don't do this because of him."

"This isn't about anyone but you and me."

A door opens and Quinn walks out, holding a long stick labelled 'bathroom pass'. She stops several yards away from us and stares, eyebrows up, glaring at Trevor.

"Syd?" Her concerned eyes dart back and forth between Trevor and me. "Everything okay?"

Trevor isn't even looking in her direction, much less bothering with the fake smile he had plastered on this morning.

"Everything's fine, Quinnlette." I use the name that only her older brother calls her. I know she hates it. I do it subconsciously, but she knows something is up when I do.

"Right," she says, not buying it. She starts walking towards us.

"No, seriously, I'm just not feeling well. Trevor was about to take me home," I say. I flash what I hope will be a convincing smile and she stops.

"Okay, well …" She gives me a long, calculating look. "I hope you feel better."

I nod and she wanders off down the hall.

"Can we please do this later?" I ask Trevor.

He looks at me and his eyes are empty.

"Whatever you say, Sydney." I silently grieve for the way his stunning blue eyes used to make me feel. If I could just get a fleeting glance of the guy he was before, I might second-guess my decision.

"I just think that it's best. For now."

"Well, if that's what you think. I think you're going to regret it. But, hey, your call."

"We'll talk in a few days?"

Nothing.

"Okay, well, I guess I'm gonna go."

I turn away from him. I almost expect to be yanked back and told not to walk away from him. I expect to be stopped. I expect the argument to continue. But he doesn't. *It* doesn't.

I leave campus. Knowing one thing for certain.

School and gym are no longer on the agenda.

Twenty-three

I spend an hour arguing with Maisy, trying to explain why she cannot have her group of friends over to stay both Friday and Saturday night. She totally ignores the note from our dad and tells me that she can do whatever she wants. She makes a big production of stomping around and slamming doors before coming downstairs to find out what we're having for dinner.

I'm upstairs trying to organise my room when the pizza arrives.

"Maisy!" I yell. "There's money by the door, can you get that?"

I'm half under my bed trying to fish out stray shoes and other odds and ends. No response, naturally. Another knock at the door.

"Ugh," I groan. I shove myself out from under the bed. My knee-length pajama pants and white tank top are now covered in a thick layer of dust from under my bed. I glance into Maisy's room as I run down the hall. She's on the phone, of course.

I yank the front door open, and then, take a quick step back. Not pizza.

Grant.

He's leaning patiently against the doorframe, dressed casually in dark grey trousers and a plain v-neck t-shirt. God, he manages to look effortless and gorgeous all at the same time.

"Hey," I say, clearly taken aback by his presence.

"Hi. Sorry to show up without calling." He seems nervous. It's so uncharacteristic of him that it's kind of endearing.

I laugh to camouflage my surprise. "I just thought you were the pizza."

"If it helps, I did bring food." He holds up a large white paper bag. "Jules has been cooking like crazy. With mom coming in tomorrow, you know. Anyway, with you and your sister here alone, I figured you could use something to eat. But, if you have food coming . . ."

"Please, there's never enough food with that kid around. That was really sweet of you."

We stand there awkwardly for a moment. Before I stop being so damn inept and invite him in. He sets the bag on the kitchen counter and opens his mouth to say something, just as there's another knock on the door.

"Hold that thought, I'll just be a second." I hold my finger up and race out of the room. I cannot *believe* that he's here. My heart is hammering loudly in my chest. In my ears. All through me. I pay for the pizza and pause momentarily outside of the kitchen to calm myself.

"Okay, sorry about that," I say. I set the box on the stove. I should call Maisy down and tell her that the food is here. I should . . . but first, I should thank Grant, right? Manners are more important.

"So, thanks for the food. That was really thoughtful."

"You're welcome. Honestly, it was my excuse to come by. You left school early, and I was worried." He speaks slowly, trying to gauge my reaction before finishing. "I couldn't stop thinking about you. I just . . . needed to know if you were all right." His hands are shoved deep in his pockets. It's an atypical stance for him – he usually radiates confidence.

"I'm fine," I say. I inspect my nails. That's a safe thing to do. Safer than looking him in the eyes, anyway.

"Look, I know it's not my place, Syd. I know that you love *him* . . . I know that you want *him*." His words are pained. "And I understand if you want me to leave. But I just had to see for myself that you weren't hurt."

I lean against the cool countertop, unsure how to respond. I'm not sure that I love Trevor anymore. I don't think I want him. And here's Grant, standing in front of me, wanting to know if *I'm* hurt, when he so obviously is *because* of me.

"I don't have a clue what I want."

He nods. "That's understandable. I know you're going through a lot, Syd. I don't mean to be unfair, or pile anymore crap on you." He takes a few slow steps to close the space in between us.

"You're not," I lie. He is. Every movement he takes away from me aches. But every step he takes towards me confuses me. My heart rate picks up again as he inches closer. He reaches for my hand and lightly strokes it with his fingertips.

"I just want you to be safe. And okay. And I can see that you aren't."

"I told you, I'm fine." I can't concentrate on anything right now. Not with him this close to me.

"What the heck?" Maisy's voice cuts through the intensity as she stomps into the kitchen. I should have heard her coming. I jerk my hand away from Grant's and spin towards Maisy.

"Hey, pizza's here!" I say. My voice cracks with all of the nerves and other emotion spinning around in me.

"Obviously. Who's this?" she asks. She nods in Grant's direction.

"This is my friend, Grant. From school," I say. Grant smiles politely at her, but she only scoffs in response.

"Friend. Right," she mumbles under her breath. She pops open the pizza boxes and pokes at the pies like they're completely foreign. "So, what's in the bags?"

Grant doesn't miss a beat and starts unpacking the food he brought over.

"We've got chicken kabobs, baked ziti and chocolate mousse," he says. Now he's speaking Maisy's language.

Maisy's eyes light up and she abandons the cardboard pizza boxes in favour of Grant's buffet.

"Are you staying for dinner?" I ask. Do I sound as eager as I feel?

"Only if you'd like," he says with a handsome smirk.

"Yes, please."

"Friends!" Maisy snorts as she piles food onto her plate.

The three of us arrange our plates on the coffee table and turn on a movie. Honestly, I don't remember the last time that I ate a meal with Maisy. On purpose. But she and Grant are getting along great. They talk about school and the movies and joke. It's more happiness than I've seen from her in months, and I have Grant to thank for it. I lean back against the sofa and listen and smile. Especially on Maisy's birthday weekend, it feels like a gift.

When the movie ends, Maisy hurries to clean up her dishes and rushes out of the room to make a call.

"You don't have to leave, Maze," I assure her.

"I know. I have to call Darla," she says.

"It was cool to meet you, Maisy. Happy birthday!" Grant says.

"You too, dude," Maisy says. "And thanks. Are you going to be coming over again?"

Grant smirks. "You'll have to ask your sister that."

They bump fists before she turns and sprints up the staircase.

"Just give me a second." I excuse myself to follow my sister.

"What's up, Syd?" Maisy asks. She's already on her bed, phone in hand.

"I just … I don't want you to think …" I have no idea what I'm trying to say.

"That you have two boyfriends?" she asks.

I let out a high-pitched, nervous laugh.

"Exactly." I nod. "Grant and I are just friends."

"Whatever, Syd. He's cool. I like him."

"I do, too," I confess. Too much.

"So, he's going to be coming over more?" she asks.

I rub my hand over the quilt on her bed. My grandmother made it for my mom a zillion years ago. What would either one of them think of what's going on in my life right now?

"I don't know what's going to happen," I say honestly.

"Oh." She reaches for her phone again. "Well, your business." She's already scrolling through her phone. I guess that's my cue to leave.

When I get back downstairs, I'm surprised to see Grant's spot on the couch vacant.

My stomach drops. No way had he left without saying goodbye. I peek into the kitchen and he's standing near the sink, drying a plate. All of the food is put away, and it looks like he's drying the last of the dishes.

Unbelievable.

"You really didn't need to do all of that," I say.

He turns around and tosses the dish towel onto the counter. He pushes a piece of hair up out of his face and grins.

"You know, you sure tell people what they should and shouldn't do a whole lot." He winks. And I'm a goner.

"Well, thanks. I haven't seen Maisy that talkative in a really long time. She must really like you."

"Does it run in the family?" he smirks. "I'm kidding, don't answer that. She's a great kid."

I swallow. And then I do a mental countdown to work up my nerve.

5 ... 4 ... 3 ... 2 ... Talk.

"Do you want to stay for a while?"

Grant nods and follows me back into the living room. There's some old 70s game show rerun on that I have zero interest in. But there's no way I could concentrate on anything anyway, so I don't bother looking for something better. Still, we both sit there. Quiet. Feigning interest in the show, like a couple of middle-schoolers on their first date.

"So, my mom mentioned they're going to pick up shooting of your show in the next week or so, right? Are you okay with that?"

"Yep," I say. I pull my hair back and twist it into a knot on the back of my head.

"I mean, I just worry that ..." Grant doesn't finish.

Drama. Trevor. Yeah, I get it.

"You worry a lot," I say.

"Sorry 'bout that." He smiles.

He reaches over and tucks a piece of hair that's already fallen from the loose knot back behind my ear. And it's then, when the familiar goosebumps cover me, that I realise how much I've come to crave it.

I suck up my nerves and rearrange myself so that I'm sitting cross-legged facing him. Only a few inches separate us now.

Breathe.

"I'm sorry you had to see all of that today. I'm so freaking embarrassed." I try my hardest not to look away from him. To maintain that constant eye contact that he specialises in.

"You don't have anything to be sorry for."

He runs his thumb along my arm.

Breathe.

"Yeah, I really do. Trevor shouldn't have caused a scene like that. And I shouldn't have let you get so involved."

"The thing is, I want to be involved. If you're a part of something, I want to be there. I can't for the life of me understand why you're even involved with that guy, but I can't change your mind. It doesn't mean that I don't want to be there for you, though."

164

"I can't ask you to do that." I finally have to look away.

"Sydney," he breathes. The way he says it and the warmth of his breath inundate me. There's so much emotion behind those two syllables. I can't make sense of how he does it. Grant leans in and wraps his hand around the back of my neck, his long fingers tickle and tangle the baby fine hairs. Softly, he pulls my face in towards his and rests his chin on my forehead.

"You'd never have to *ask* for anything from me. I'd do anything for you. Willingly, you know? And then some."

He tips his head slightly and presses his lips to my forehead. They're warm and electric. But it's his words that stun me. Wrap around me. Leaving me tumbly and shaky with an inexplicable longing. I don't think about what I'm doing for once. I don't calculate risk. Or weigh options. I don't think about deductions for imperfect form. I just do it.

I press my lips to his. At first he's frozen. But it only takes a second before his mouth and the rest of him reacts. He pulls me in by my hips and crushes his mouth onto mine. It's warm and intense and everything I'd expected it to be. And better. All of the months of pent-up attraction and fascination collide, and the result is nothing short of exhilarating.

His grip on my hip is firm and protective, without feeling possessive. It's so different from what I've experienced before. He parts my lips gently and his warm breath fills my mouth. One of his hands moves to my face and the other rests just under my tank top on the bare skin of my back.

This is a completely new feeling. Even with Trevor, I never experienced this level of desire. Something about our connection is so different. It's just so much more than physical with Grant. But the physical stuff is amazing. Right now, in this moment, in these arms, I understand just how hard I'd been fighting it.

I lean back on the sofa and pull Grant down on top of me without releasing his lips. He lets out a low, soft moan and positions himself carefully so that he isn't actually putting any weight on me. I wouldn't care if he was. I *want* to be near him.

He unlocks his lips from mine and moves them to my neck. My entire body is tingling at the feeling of his mouth on my skin. I don't ever want it to stop. I wonder if he has any idea how amazing it feels to be so close to him. Or how good he is at what he's doing. He moves his lips to my collar bone and, from there, down the length of my arm. The kisses are slow and he intertwines one of his hands in mine. The other slips up the back of my shirt, pressing me closer to him. Grant's hand slinks around to my stomach, up onto my breasts and I gasp against his mouth as his thumb grazes over my nipple. A thousand nerve endings I didn't know exists ignite. And something else, something I thought I'd felt but pales in comparison to what I'm feeling for Grant right now – desire. I want him. It's so completely different from the way Trevor touched me. Grants hands move in a way that prove that he's doing it because he wants to touch me, he wants to make me feel good, I'm not a possession to him. It's amazing, and I want to beg him to never stop.

"Sydney," he sighs. He's stopped kissing me, but the room is still spinning. He's not holding me anymore, but is sitting on the floor, kneeling right beside me on the sofa, but he might as well be a continent away now.

"What's the matter?" I ask self-consciously.

He exhales sharply. "We can't do this."

"What? Why not?" My insecurity takes over and the room comes to an abrupt halt.

"Trust me, there's nothing I'd rather do." He leans in and kisses the top of my nose. I won't look at him. "But you've got to figure out

166

what you want for yourself. I told you, I don't want to complicate things, and that's exactly what *this* is doing."

Please stop trying to be a good guy and just go back to kissing me.

"I don't want to stop." I let the words tumble out before I can stop them. He lets out a deep chuckle, because apparently my honesty is amusing.

"You have no idea how much I don't want you to." He breathes in my ear. His voice is nearly hypnotising me again.

"Did I do something wrong?" I ask.

"Sydney, be serious. I've made it completely clear how I feel about you. I'd like nothing more than to be able to kiss you every second of everyday. And then some. But you need to make up your mind about what you want. And *who* you want. I'm not going to be the other guy in this situation." He's still holding my hand and rubbing it along the side of his face.

But he cheats on his own rules and lightly kisses my ear, causing the pleasure-filled vertigo to return.

"Will you at least stay with me tonight? I mean, just sleep?" I ask. I don't even recognise my own voice.

He doesn't respond right away. He just looks at me, thinking about what the right thing to do is. He's forever trying to do the right thing.

When he speaks, he sounds unsure, and maybe a little pained.

"I would kill to be able to wake up next to you in the morning, Syd. But with Maisy here … it's just not the best idea." It dawns on me that it's actually hard on him. He's trying to convince himself just as much as he's trying to convince me.

I frown, a big, childish pout.

"You're making it incredibly difficult for me to be the good guy right now," he says with a soft laugh. He lightly breezes his thumb across my pouting lip. "Let me at least get you up to bed." Grant effortlessly scoops me up into his arms. My first instinct is to argue that it's not necessary to carry me, but I decide against it. It likely wouldn't do any good, and I want to be close to him. So this time, I don't shy away from his grip on my thighs, and instead, bury myself into his strong chest and his clean, warm smell. He takes the time to walk to each of the lamps while he holds me and turn them off before heading up the stairs.

"You're going to have to point me in the right direction," he whispers. Maisy has already gone to bed, and the hallway is dark. I point to my bedroom door, the second one on the right, and Grant carries me inside, holding me as close as possible.

"So, this is your room," he says. He glances all around, taking in the trophies and photos. I cringe when he stops to inspect a photo of Trevor and me. Happy. Close. Grant doesn't flinch, or otherwise react. I get the feeling he's not intimidated by Trevor, or my relationship with him, whatever that is.

Finally, Grant carries me to my bed and sets me down. I pull my duvet up over my body. I catch his eyes drift over to the alarm clock on the nightstand and I frown, anticipating his next move.

"It's getting really late. You'd better get some sleep. Big party tomorrow, remember?" he says.

"I guess," I concede with a heavy shrug. I can already feel my eyes getting heavier now that I'm in bed. It's been a draining day.

"I'll lock the door on my way out. Call me tomorrow."

I nod and let my eyes close. I feel the warmth of his lips on my forehead. I can't even dream anything this good.

Twenty-four

The next day is one of those busy days that leave you euphoric from having been so productive. Maisy and I clean the house, grocery shop and rearrange the living room. Thanks to Grant breaking the ice, she and I talk more than we have in a long time.

"Hey, Syd," she says. We're folding laundry on the couch. It's nothing serious, but her face is thoughtful. "I'm sorry your plans got messed up this weekend. Sorry you have to stay with me."

I toss the t-shirt I was folding back into the wrinkled pile.

"I'm not," I say.

"And I'm sorry I've sorta been a jerk lately."

"Maisy, you haven't," I say. It's a lie. She has. But she's my sister. My only sister.

"Yeah, I really have. It's just that I get jealous of you." She's analysing three different socks to decipher which are matches.

"Why in the world would you be jealous of me?" I'm floored.

"You have everything. Gymnastics. The cool boyfriend. *Or two,*" she says with a broad smile. "And you had mom . . ."

And there it is.

"Maisy . . . I work really hard at gymnastics. That's not something that comes easy. You could do really well at things, too, if you tried. As for Mom, you're right. I feel guilty about that every single day. The boyfriend stuff, well, that's a lot more compli-cated."

She shrugs.

Maisy's friends show up later that night. Dad had talked with each of their parents before he left to let them know that he'd be out of town and it was just me at home, but still, they all came to the door to check on things, and talk about gymnastics and the show. I hate being a spectacle. I debated whether to call Quinn and Tess to come stay with me and the girls, but decided against it at the last minute. I hadn't really been a great friend to either one of them lately. I'm glad there's only a week of school left, then I'll have some more free time to devote to my friends.

Grant had said he'd be spending most of the summer in New York. I felt queasy all of a sudden at the thought of not seeing him for months. I don't have any trouble remembering the way it felt when he held me last night. Or the new brazenness I felt kissing him.

But I don't regret it. He told me to call him, but I've been putting it off all evening, waiting until Maisy and her friends were settled in for the night. I want to be able to devote my full attention to him. That doesn't stop me from counting down the hours until I could make the call and hear his voice.

I've been thinking all day about what he said about my needing to figure things out before there could be anything between me and him. I know he's right. I love Trevor. It's not as easy as Grant makes it all sound. To just walk away? I owe it to Trevor to talk to him and sort it all out once and for all. I know I should feel guilty that I'm putting him through all of this the week before his graduation, but I just can't make myself.

The girls aren't nearly as much trouble as I'd expected. For the most part, they just stay up in Maisy's room on their phones. I try to remember back to when I was thirteen, to what I did for my birthday. I can't conjure up a memory. I probably had to train or something, instead of having a party. After the girls have raided the kitchen for dessert, they quiet down enough for me to make my long-anticipated call.

It's absurd to be as nervous as I am as I dial Grant's number. He'd told me to call. As soon as the ringing starts, I realise that it's far later than I'd thought. I'm debating whether or not to just hang up when he answers.

"Sydney!" His voice is full of delight. I can almost see his smile through the phone. Brightening his entire face and crinkling the skin around his eyes.

"I'm sorry to call so late," I say softly, trying to disguise the girlish enthusiasm in my voice.

"I was up," he says. "How's the party?"

"It's been good. I think Maisy's having a good time." I should feel awkward after last night. After I begged him to stay with me. But it feels too good to be uncomfortable. "Did your mom make it in okay?"

"Yeah, she sure did." The line goes quiet. He wants to say more, but he's chosen not to.

"Grant?" I ask.

"I told my mom about you," he says. "I mean, I told her that you're more than just some girl at school."

My heart starts to pound so hard I can feel the thump, thump, thump of the blood in my ears.

"Me? Why?" I imagine him shrugging on the other end of the line.

"Because you're important."

I'm not sure how to follow up a comment like that. He's better at this than I am. I feel like no matter what I say, it won't be an adequate enough expression of how I really feel.

"I'm glad you came by last night," I say. I can't declare my true feelings yet. Not until I talk to Trevor. My indecisiveness hasn't been fair to anyone. So I swallow hard and bury the words I want to say.

There's a rustling noise. I can't tell if it's coming through the phone, or if it's in the house. I tense up as I listen for it again. Every muscle is tight. I'm such a wimp. I can't believe Dad left me in charge.

"Do you hear that?" I ask Grant.

"Hear what?" So, no, not on his end.

"Nothing, I just heard something in the house."

There it is again.

"Do you need me to come over?" *A tempting suggestion.*

"No, it's probably just Maisy." I want to accept his offer, but I'm sure it's nothing, and it is super late.

I hear a different noise, louder this time.

"Hey, I've got to let you go. I need to check on the girls." I hate to end this conversation.

"Syd?" Grant sounds worried. "Call me back if you need anything."

I tiptoe down the hall and peer around the top of the stairs to investigate the source of the noise. I'm not the least bit brave, and while I'm confident there isn't an intruder, I'm still uneasy. I slowly walk down the steps, wishing I'd thought to grab some sort of makeshift weapon. Just in case. All I have in my hand is my iPhone, and that likely won't do me much good in a struggle.

There are hushed movements as I turn the corner into the kitchen. I hold my breath and flip on the light.

"Maisy, you have got to be kidding me," I say. There, halfway out the kitchen door, stand nine girls, looking like ninjas and dressed from head to toe in black clothing, each holding a large package of toilet paper.

I snatch the pack from Maisy's grip.

"Oh, come on, Syd! You did the same thing when you were our

age!" Her friends look around nervously. I have to laugh at their terrified expressions; most of them are bigger than me.

"Actually, no, I didn't," I corrected. I can't think of a single time I'd ever gone toilet-papering. I wonder if I'd missed out on anything. In any case, I can't, in good conscience, let the girls out of the house.

"Sorry, girls. It's not gonna happen."

They hang their heads, and Maisy shoots me the stabby eyes that I'd almost missed with all of our friendly banter the last two days. They trudge back upstairs like prisoners and I follow behind to grab a pillow and blanket from my bed. Sleeping on the sofa is the best option for the night; there's no way they'd dare try to sneak out again with me right there.

I stretch out comfortably on the long couch and turn on a movie. *Love Actually*, my all-time favourite. I recite the lines in my head as I doze in and out of sleep while the familiar faces flicker across the screen.

"Sydney," I hear the faintest whisper of my name and the tickle of warm breath on my ear.

Someone *is* in the house this time. I shoot upright in a panic.

Trevor is sitting next to me on the sofa, a thin, tight smile on his face. *How did he get in here?* It takes me a minute to remember the incident with the toilet paper. I must have forgotten to lock the door behind Maisy and her friends earlier. I squint to see the time on the DVD player, but my eyes are still too heavy with sleep to make it out.

"What are you doing here?" I ask. Honestly, I'm surprised I haven't heard from him at all this weekend, but I didn't expect him to show up like this, in the middle of the night.

"I missed you," Trevor says. He strokes a light line down my arm with his fingertip. "I couldn't sleep – couldn't stop thinking about you."

"What time is it?" I ask. He looks around the room as if he

doesn't know, or particularly care and doesn't answer me. "Wait, you drove all the way from the lake?"

He nods. I should feel flattered. Important. Loved. Instead, I'm annoyed. I'm not prepared for this right now. I asked for some time, and he isn't going to allow me that.

Trevor leans in and kisses my neck. It's rough and feels wrong. I can't help it; I tense up at his touch and I'm positive he's aware of the change in my posture. He pulls back slightly and measures my expression. Then ignores it. Because it's obvious he isn't here for me. He wraps his arms around my waist and pulls me in close to him. His lips press into mine. Intensely. Full of hunger. With something to prove. The feeling of his tongue in my mouth causes an unexpected wave of disgust to overtake me.

"It's late, Trevor," I say. I try to snake around him.

"But we're alone," he says. He isn't backing off.

"Not even close," I correct. "There are almost a dozen kids upstairs." He isn't bothered by this fact, and presses himself to me, pinning me to the couch.

"That just means we have to be quiet," he says with a devilish smirk.

His hands move across my skin, over my stomach, along my collar bone, in a way that used to thrill me, but now, I cringe.

"We need to talk," I say. I try to push him off of me, but he isn't concerned with my lack of interest.

"I don't want to *talk*, Sydney. I *want* you."

I'm so caught off guard that it takes little effort for him to restrain me and he easily pins my wrists above my head with one hand. He kisses my throat aggressively; the stubble from his unshaven cheeks rubs my neck raw and makes me recoil.

"Seriously, Trevor, please stop." My voice is more panicked than I'd anticipated.

"I need you," he says.

My mind is racing. I can feel my throat tightening up. *Why didn't I lock the door? How did this person that I had loved so wholeheartedly, turn into someone that I'm totally terrified of?*

"Please," I beg.

I doubt that I could scream, even if I wanted to. I never would, of course. I'd never want Maisy to walk in and see me like this. One of his hands presses on my thigh, while the other slides under my tank top.

"But I love you, Syd." *I just want him off of me. Just get off of me.*

"But, I don't love you." The words are stunning, even to my own ears as they tumble out of my mouth.

Trevor jerks back; his crystal clear blue eyes are wide with surprise. His movement creates a small enough gap for me to slide out from under him and I scramble up and stand on the opposite side of the room.

"I'm sorry, what?"

"I told you that I needed some time," I whisper. I'm trying to keep my voice low so Maisy doesn't come down, but, also, I can't muster up anything bigger.

"And I gave it to you," he says, categorically.

"No, not really," I say, staring at my intertwined fingers.

He works his jaw back and forth.

"So, that's it?"

"I – I guess so."

I can already hear the stories about how crazy I am for breaking up with someone so perfect. Or, maybe they'll spin them to say that Trevor left me. No one would be the least bit surprised by that.

"I could have done so much better," he says callously. My gaze darts to him. He's shaking his head, and his lips curve into a thin smirk. "I can't believe I wasted so much time with you."

175

I can't believe he's turning what we had into something so meaningless. I can't respond. I just stand there, frozen in the middle of the living room. The TV continues to flicker the opening sequence to the movie over and over. A large, red heart covers the screen. I'm terrified. I'm angry. I'm breaking. But the irony of the heart in this situation makes me crack the smallest of nervous smiles.

Trevor catches it.

"Are you laughing at me?" He steps closer.

"No," I say meekly. I look back down at my hands again. "I think you should go."

He continues toward me until I'm cornered against the wall. He hasn't even touched me, but I immediately have to take smaller breaths. I look around him for an exit as I try to calm myself to make breathing easier.

"Are you *seriously* laughing at me?" His forehead presses against mine. His eyes are locked on mine.

I shake my head.

"Who do you think you are, Sydney? You're nothing. Do you think you're special because of the whole gymnastics bit? You lost, remember? Or your stupid TV show? Or that people should feel sorry for you because your mom died? Because I'll tell you something, nobody gives a damn about any of that – or you. You were nothing before me. Nothing." He laughs a low, malicious scoff. I've never heard anything like it.

I feel my legs start to shake. They're strong, but they are going to give out. I'm sure of it.

I *try* to speak. I try to tell him that he's right. I am nothing. *Just please go.* But I can't. My lips won't cooperate.

His eyes narrow and his rage is growing, even though I haven't said a word.

"Wait a second. You're already involved with that asshole, aren't

176

you? That's why you think you're the shit all of a sudden." He reaches up and his hand presses on my airway.

I stare at him. Blankly. Because what else can I do? I need to lie. *Deny, I tell myself. Just deny it.* But I'm too paralysed by fear to do anything. I stand where I am. Mute. Defenseless.

He tugs violently on my arm and flings me to the floor, not like the ball of muscle that I actually am, but like a ragdoll. I gasp from the pain as my face smacks into the hard wood floor. Our eyes lock again. I know that, despite all of his anger, the Trevor I'd originally loved is in there somewhere. And, as if on cue, his face softens a bit.

"I'm sorry," I whimper.

"Syd—"

"I'm really sorry things turned out this way," I say. I'm dazed from the pounding in my head. This must be what it feels like to be the bad kind of drunk, when it's not fun anymore.

"I'm sorry, too, baby. I just want things to get back to the way they were before he came along and ruined everything." Trevor reaches his hand out for me. He's obviously misinterpreted my apology.

"No," I whisper. He cocks his head to the side in confusion. "We can't go back, Trevor. And right now, I just need you to go." I start to get up off the floor, but am knocked back down almost instantly by a fist to my face. I feel like my body is deflating. The pain is so staggering and so unexpected.

I can't be sure whether I lost consciousness or not. You don't pass out from a single punch, do you? Still, it feels like a lot of time has passed since I heard the front door close.

My face is throbbing. The room is swirly and I can't stop the sound of blood pounding in my ears. I don't have the energy to find a mirror to inspect the damage, and really, I don't care. I know I'm a mess. I feel like there's a massive weight on my chest, making it impossible to take anything but tiny, shallow breaths.

I drag myself to the other side of the room. My iPhone is still on the coffee table where I'd left it after Maisy's attempt at sneaking out. Could that have really just been a few hours ago? I think about calling Quinn, but it's too much to have to explain. I can't call Dad, he'd go crazy. I start to dial Grant's number; he's the one person that I won't have to explain anything to. He'll just be here. But just as I start to dial, the room starts to spin again. I send him a quick text before everything goes black.

It's simple. To the point. Just like Grant had been in his card with the pearls. I know he'll understand.

Mercy.

Twenty-five

Grant helps me to my bed and props a pillow up behind me.

"All right, Quinn says Maisy can stay with her as long as you need. And your dad—"

"Did you tell my dad?" I ask. I rub my temples, trying to soothe the ache in my head. It doesn't help.

"The hospital had to call to get authorisation to treat you, Syd. I don't know what they told him."

"But he's coming home, right?" I ask.

Grant nods. I can't believe this is my life.

"What am I going to tell him?" I ask.

He puckers his brow. "Why not the truth?"

I wish it were that simple. The truth is ugly. And embarrassing.

He reaches over and his hands cover mine, taking over for me, rubbing my head softly. His touch *does* help take the edge off and I finally close my eyes.

"You don't know how hard it is for me to sit here and look at you like this and not go and find him . . ." He lets his incensed voice trail off when he feels me stiffen.

"He didn't mean to," I say softly. I really do believe that he didn't intentionally hurt me like this.

"Syd, don't you *dare* defend him."

"I'm sorry," I whisper. I can't hold on to the tears anymore, and finally, I let them fall.

"You don't have anything to apologise for," he murmurs. "*He* hit you. He gave you a concussion. You didn't do anything wrong." His voice is soft again.

"I shouldn't have dragged you into this."

"Stop." We both stay quiet for a long time, until finally Grant clears his throat and speaks again.

"What happened, Sydney?"

I close my eyes and try to put the pieces together. I remember waking up and Trevor was there. I remember him backing me into the corner, but I can't fully recall what sparked the argument.

"I don't really remember."

"I can't believe that he did this to you, Syd." Grant's shaking his head in disgust.

I bite my lip nervously. "Please don't go after him."

"I'm not leaving you." It's not a promise that he won't go and find Trevor later, and it doesn't go unnoticed.

"When I found you lying on the floor, seeing you like that . . ."

"How did you know to come over?"

"You texted me." He holds up his phone as proof. Now I remember. The text. Me conceding that I couldn't do it anymore.

"You can't go back to him."

"I know."

"I'm serious, Sydney, I know I said that I'd be here for you, and I will, but I really don't know how to sit by knowing that you're in danger . . ." his voice trails off as the door opens.

Dad.

Twenty-six

Quinn sits behind me on my bed, intricately braiding my hair while we watch TV. We're watching a ridiculous reality show that does little to distract me. It reminds me of the show that I was supposed to be a part of. The one I had to drop out of – Dad's orders. Nothing that would cause me any stress for a while, he said. Luckily, Grant and his 'connections' made it a little easier to deal with.

Quinn has been here day and night since 'it' happened. Telling Quinn about Trevor had been easier than telling my Dad. Of course she was shocked, even though she'd been perceptive enough to realise that there was something off about Trevor from the beginning. She couldn't understand why I didn't confide her. We'd been friends since we were kids and have never kept secrets. I think that my silence hurt her more than she lets on.

"I have something for you, although I'm not sure that you'll want it," Quinn says as she wraps a rubber band around the end of the braid.

"What is it?" I ask, eyeing her nervously.

She crosses the room and grabs her backpack. She reaches inside and pulls out a thick, hardcover burgundy book and hands it to me. My yearbook.

"I had everyone sign it for you," she says.

181

"Thank you," I say. "That was really awesome of you to do, you know, with you hating people and all." I smile.

"You know it!" Quinn laughs.

I set the book on the bed next to me. I'm not sure I'm ready to remember the last school year. It had started out with such promise, and ended so abysmally.

"Hey, Syd," Quinn starts. "Can I ask you something?"

"Course."

"I can't stop thinking about this, and I know you don't want to talk about it, but why didn't you fight back? You're like the strongest chick I know. I mean, hello, those abs? You totally could've taken him. Hell, I would've done it for you!"

I force a small smile for her benefit.

"I just couldn't," I say. "I don't know how to explain it. I just froze. I was too scared and too shocked, and just ... paralysed."

"I wish you would've told me."

"Yeah, me too." I run my hand across the bumpy cover of the yearbook. "So, how are things at school?" I'm purposely being vague.

"I kept my promise, if that's what you're asking – I didn't say anything to him."

"Thank you."

"Hey, I can behave when I have to, no matter what you've heard!" She grins.

"How ..." I struggle with the next question. I have to know, but I know that she won't like it. "How is he?"

"Syd." She hesitates. I nod, urging her to go on. "He's *Trevor*. He's fine, I guess. He's been acting normal. Or at least like nothing is bothering him at all."

That doesn't surprise me in the least. He's able to continue with his normal life, while I'm stuck up in my room. Missing gym. Going to therapy.

"Thanks."

"Listen, I hate to do this to you, but I've got to run home and grab a couple of things."

"Sure."

"I'll be back in, like, an hour tops, though. You'll be alright?"

"Yes, Quinny, I'm totally fine. Get out of here."

I can't wait for Dad to decide I can go back to gym. I just want normal. I'm so tired of feeling so helpless. I've spent the last year feeling this way.

"Sydney."

I pull myself up. "Oh, hey, Dad."

"Listen, Syd, I thought about what you said about pressing charges. And you have to understand, I'm your father—"

I cut him off.

"Dad, please. Please don't make me go through that. *Please.* I just want to forget that this year ever happened. How am I supposed to do that if I'm forced to go through all that?"

"I know, Syd. I know you're scared. But my job is to protect you."

"I'm not scared. And you *have* protected me. If I file a formal complaint, everyone is going to find out. *Everyone.* It could totally sabotage my gymnastics career, not to mention my senior year of high school." Dad frowns at me, but I'm not finished. "Look, Trevor will be leaving in a few weeks for school and I'll never see him again."

Dad lets out a long sigh.

"All right, Syd. If this is what you need to help you move on, we'll play by your rules." I know this has to be hard on him. After losing my mom, and then seeing me hurt, he's been through a lot.

"Get some rest," he pats my knee and I feel like I'm twelve and home sick with the flu.

I lie back down and close my eyes. I haven't heard from Grant all week. I'd be lying if I said it didn't tear at my heart a little. He gave me advance warning at least that he'd be lying low, that he wanted to give me some space, and time to clear my head. But I don't feel like I need it. I don't want to be away from him. And I've spent the last several months feeling so uncertain about everything. I just don't feel that anymore.

Although Dad is rightfully cautious about another guy in my life, he's really taken to Grant and seems indebted to him once I'd explained how he'd helped me.

"Sydney." The nearby whisper terrifies me. I bite my bottom lip to stop its quivering. My eyes fly open.

"I'm sorry. I didn't mean to wake you," Grant says softly. He's standing near the foot of the bed, unshaven, unruly hair and a plain t-shirt. Just the way I like him.

"You didn't wake me. I was just ... you scared me," I admit.

His eyes flash with a mixture of anger and regret. He never did confront Trevor, at least not that I know of. It's left him conflicted; he wants to do what I say will make me happy, but everything in him is telling him to make Trevor pay.

"Right. I'm sorry."

"Sit." I pat the bed lightly and he takes a seat next to me.

"You look good, Syd." *Translation: no more swollen jaw. No more black eye.* "I've missed you."

"What's the matter?" I ask quietly.

"I just ..." He's having trouble saying whatever it is that he came to say. I feel myself start to tense up.

"It's okay. I understand," I say.

"Understand what?"

"I understand that it's just too much. Me ... all of this, it's too much for you. I get it, and trust me, I don't blame you." And I really don't. I've put this guy through hell.

"Not even close, Syd. I've already told you, I want you. You *have* to know that I want you more than anything. But I want you to *want* to be with me."

"I *do want* to be with you," I respond quickly.

"The thing is, I don't want you to fall into another relationship just because it's here or it's easy. You need to worry about making yourself happy first. You try so hard to please everyone else all of the time and it just can't go on like that."

I know what I want. He's sitting right in front of me. But what he just said makes him sound like a parrot on my therapist's shoulder. Which likely means that he's right. Damn.

"I need for you to be sure that it's what you really want. I don't want you to second-guess yourself and think you moved too quickly once we were together." He laces his fingers through mine. They are a perfect fit.

His eyes are thoughtful as he continues. "I don't know if I'd be able to let you go once I had you, Sydney."

His words are too much. The emotion tearing through me is like nothing I've experienced before.

"Then why did you come today?" I ask.

He looks around the room. The walls are barer than the last time he was here. No prom photos, no gifts from Trevor on display.

"What is it?" I push.

"I came to say goodbye." Grant's words make me have to stop and catch my breath. "I'm leaving to stay with my brother in New York tomorrow."

"How long are you going to be gone?" My voice is cracking.

"Two months." *Two months?* Two whole months without those eyes? That messy, perfect hair? That smile that cures everything and makes me trust like nothing else?

"I don't want you to go," I whimper. I bite my lip and consider my next question.

"What is it?" he asks. He leans over and nips at my bottom lip, turning the pout into a grin.

"So, does what you said about wanting to kiss me every time we're together still stand?"

He doesn't hesitate.

"It does now. It will when I get back."

And he kisses me. Softly at first, and then, cupping my face in his long hands and really, really kissing me. Melting every bit of doubt and sadness in me.

"So, I'm supposed to take all this time apart to convince you that I do, in fact, want you. What if *you* don't want *me* by then?"

He laughs softly. "That won't happen."

"But how do you *know*?" I press.

His face becomes more serious and he looks away from me briefly, as if he's collecting his thoughts.

"Because, I love you, Sydney. I can't just turn that off." He says it so matter-of-fact that I'm certain I stop breathing.

I shake my head. He tilts my chin up with his index finger so that I'm looking at him. *Always*. Because with Grant, it's all out in the open. It's all sincere. There's nothing fake, and nothing to hide from.

"What?" he asks.

I wrack my brain for the right words. I don't know how to explain what I'm feeling.

"I just, I can't believe that you feel that way," I stumble over my words.

"Why?" he asks. "I've never made it a secret. I've loved you from day one."

"I just … I …" It's too hard to form a thought with him this close to me.

He leans in even closer, and his lips brush against my ear.

"Sydney, I love you," he breathes, his warm breath ruffling my hair. He rubs his nose along my ear and a chill runs through me.

"I—" I start. I want to tell him that I love him too, but he presses his index finger to my lips and shakes his head.

"Shhh …" he says with a slight smile. "You know that day with the joke with the glow sticks? When I said that you were delicate?" He runs his finger along my jaw and kisses me gently. I don't know where he's going with this, but I nod. "Well, you're not. You're so strong, Syd."

I shake my head. "No, no I'm not. If I were, I would've told someone, I would have gotten out sooner."

"*You are.* Do I wish you would've left him a long time ago? Hell yeah. But there's something to be said for someone brave enough to take on that kind of darkness alone. You've already made it through so much, and you'll make it through this, too. But it can't be because of me. It has to come from you. No matter how much I just want to hold you, and protect you. I'll be here waiting, though."

Two months …

Epilogue

I slept through most of the flight. I've never travelled alone before, I always have Dad or Sam with me, but I'm sort of surprised with how at ease I've been. I've been training really hard at gym ever since I got the okay from the doctors and Dad, and it'd left me exhausted in the best way, so sleep came easily. I was glad to be back in a normal routine though; it felt good.

I'm amazed at how quickly the summer flew by. After such a terrible start, I expected that it would drag on. I kept busy with gym once I was able to go back, and hung out with Quinn and Tessa a lot. It was nice to have my friends back. To be able to joke with them, and act stupidly, without a dark secret looming over me. The best part was that me, Dad and Maisy had finally taken a family holiday. We hadn't done that since Mom died. We went to Oregon to visit Mom's family, who we rarely ever saw.

I felt so at peace in my mom's childhood home. I stayed up late, in the room that she'd grown up in. I felt close to her, like she was helping to guide me. And, strangely, being in a town of total strangers was exactly what I needed to find myself again. I realised that I was okay, just as I was. That everything didn't have to be perfect all the time. That I didn't have to make everyone happy, and the only person's happiness that I was responsible for was my own.

So, that's where I'm headed; *to my happiness.*

Grant and I had talked daily since he left for New York. He'd sent me e-mails full of gorgeous photos and packages of trinkets that he'd pick up. Our nightly phone conversations had become my favourite part of the day. We could *and would* talk about everything under the sun.

And this trip? This is my birthday present to *myself.* Dad and Quinn were shocked when I didn't want to have a big eighteenth birthday party. I had something else in mind.

I knew that just like I had been with his, Grant was totally in the dark about when my birthday was. The idea occurred to me while I was in Oregon. I stopped by to visit Julie when I got back from my vacation with Maisy and Dad and she helped me plan my trip.

I'd cleaned out my savings account and was going to surprise Grant. I could perfectly appreciate how he felt when he said that he'd spent his birthday exactly how he wanted when he'd spent it with me.

We're landing and still, the nerves that had once been so paralysing have yet to kick in. Instead, I feel completely serene and at peace with my decisions. I grab my carryon bag from under the seat and follow the crowd off of the plane. I keep waiting for the claustrophobia to strike, but it never comes.

Julie made arrangements for someone to pick me up from the airport. If I had any idea where I was going, I probably would have jumped out of the car and run down the streets myself. The traffic is like nothing I've ever seen. I admit, my stomach tightens when the driver stops outside a massive building and the doorman helps me with my bags.

I've made it this far, all expertly planned by Julie, but now, I'm on my own.

I start wringing my hands as the elevator climbs floors. I pull the address card out of my purse and read it for the hundredth time. I know which apartment I'm looking for, but I keep checking constantly. Just in case. The elevator doors open and reveal a small hallway, decorated in thick, formal wallpaper. The stuffy interior makes me cringe. There's the claustrophobia I'd missed so much. But there's only one door down the hall, *Grant's door*. The apartment he's been staying with his brother in for the summer. It's right there.

I hesitate at the door. *This is it. What if he's not even home?*

I knock lightly and wait. He might not have heard the light knock; he wouldn't have been expecting it since the doorman hadn't buzzed. I raise my hand to knock again and the door flies open.

And he's there.

His hair is a little longer, a lot more unruly, and just as perfect. He's casual like always, wearing plaid shorts, a navy blue sleeveless shirt and brown leather flip flops. His face lights up and his mouth forms his trademark, flawless smile.

"Sydney!" he gasps. He doesn't even hesitate and instead, pulls me up off of the ground and close to him.

"What are you doing here?" His eyes are wide with surprise.

I smile widely at him. "It's *my* birthday."

He's still holding me tightly. He holds me high enough that I'm eye-level with him, my feet dangling high off the ground. He kicks the door shut behind him and carries me to the couch.

The inside of the apartment is formal, like the halls. It's spotless and a little stuffy, but Grant's laid-back vibe helps balance it all out.

"This is amazing," I say. The view from the floor to ceiling windows is something I'd only imagined ever seeing. Skyscrapers and famous landmarks for as far as I could see.

He sits down on the firm, white sofa and sets me sideways on his lap. He reaches up and brushes my hair back behind my shoulders.

"I can't believe that you're here," he says.

"Well, it's been a lot of days without kisses," I say.

He laughs quietly and pulls me closer. He teases me with his lips, brushing them across my cheeks, my lips, and my forehead. Never staying anywhere long enough for me to really reciprocate.

"Happy birthday," he says. He traces a line up and down my spine with his fingers and I tremble with delight.

"Thank you," I say. It's peaceful, and right, and perfect.

"So, how did you get here? I mean, how did you know where I was?"

I'd worried that Julie might slip and reveal the surprise, but it's obvious from the expression on his face that he never had a hint that I was coming.

"Julie helped." I'm sure he knew that she was capable of close to anything.

He nuzzles his nose under my ear and kisses the skin lightly. I'd missed the feeling of those lips.

"I missed you," I whisper.

"I missed you too, baby." He kisses my chin, my nose, and then finally my lips. And it's all I'd been waiting for for months. Because it isn't just a kiss. It's finally the start of us. Real and honest, and safe. I love Grant. I love him for being all of those things.

I loved Trevor wholly. In all the good ways that made me feel alive and special and important. But also, in the bad ways. The ways that shut me off from others and left me alone with my pain. The ways that had me keep secrets. I loved Trevor in all the ways that I thought mattered, even though I knew that I didn't.

Letting go is never easy. Especially when you can't see where you're going to land. But I've learned that sometimes, you just have to throw your weight behind the change. Take the chance that you may fall.

Did some cosmic force step in and bring Grant into my life at just the right time to rescue me? I don't know. The one thing that I *am* sure of is that there will be a lot more uncertainties in my life. There will always be another difficult dismount, and countless more blind landings. But for the first time in my life, I'm okay with that. I'm looking forward to the twists and turns, and surprises – there'll be a thousand more times I won't be able to see where I'm going to land.

Grant wraps his hand through mine and I know that whether I land firmly, or fall, he'll be right there, next to me.

Authors Note

Recently the NSPCC complied a report on abuse in teenage relationships, and nearly 75% of girls that responded said they had suffered some kind of emotional partner violence and 33% had experienced some kind of sexual violence.

If you've been affected by Sydney's story then there is help available. A good starting point is this website: http://thisisabuse.direct.gov.uk/home. There you'll find more information on abusive relationships as well as ways to get help if you need it.

Remember, Love is *not* abuse.

Acknowledgments

To my Lucky 21. You are, by far, the best part of this whole crazy, publishing journey. So blessed to have every single one of you in my life. Love you all.

To the amazing, hilarious and just plain awesome, Liz Reinhardt who cheered me on to the finish line. (And reads faster than anyone I know.) I owe you, gorgeous.

Thanks to my agent, Lauren Abramo, who tolerates my inane questions like no one I've ever met before. So lucky to have you in my corner.

To Nyrae Dawn, for always having the right thing to say. Whether it's a sick kid, a writing frustration, or a funny mishap. You are the definition of a true friend. xo

To Colleen Hoover, because, you know, you're a NYT Best Seller, but still, when I need a beta reader, you're all, *"send it over, I'll get it back to you today."* Rock.Star.

And, thanks to Mike, for the glow-sticks.

About the Author

Steph Campbell grew up in Southern California, but now calls Southwest Louisiana home. She has one husband, four children and a serious nail polish obsession.

Novels Currently Available by Steph Campbell are:

DELICATE (Contemporary YA)
GROUNDING QUINN (Contemporary YA Mature)
BEAUTIFUL THINGS NEVER LAST (Contemporary NA)
MY HEART FOR YOURS - with Jolene Perry (Contemporary
   NA)
LENGTHS - with Liz Reinhardt (Contemporary NA)
A TOAST TO THE GOOD TIMES - with Liz Reinhardt
   (Contemporary NA)

stephcampbell.blogspot.com/
@stephcampbell_